Reggie and Joan

ABOUT THE AUTHOR

Pelham Grenville Wodehouse was born in Guildford, England, in 1881 while his mother was visiting from Hong Kong, where his father was a colonial civil servant. She returned to the crown colony with her infant, but soon sent him back to England to be civilized for school by a nanny and two aunts.

At Dulwich College, Wodehouse's public school, he edited the magazine while excelling at cricket, rugby, and classics. After his family suffered a financial setback, he went to work for the Hong Kong and Shanghai Bank in London. He proved, in his words, "to be the most inefficient clerk whose trouser seat ever polished a stool." But a former master at Dulwich helped him get a job at the Globe newspaper and embark on a writing career that produced hundreds of works, including novels, plays, poems, short stories, and song lyrics.

Wodehouse became a United States citizen in 1955 and died on Valentine's Day in 1975.

As any Woodhousian knows, his last name rhymes with "good house," not "road house," and his friends simply called him "Plum," from his childhood pronunciation of Pelham.

Reggie and Joan

The Misadventures of Reggie Pepper

&

The Sporting Life of Joan Romney

P. G. WODEHOUSE

Rushwater Press

RUSHWATER PRESS
P.O. Box 42
Roxbury, CT 06783, USA

Edited text copyright © 2013
Patricia T. O'Conner and Stewart Kellerman
All rights reserved.

Includes editors' note and biographical sketch.

Publisher's Cataloging-in-Publication Data
Wodehouse, P. G. (Pelham Grenville), 1881-1975,
Reggie and Joan: the misadventures of Reggie Pepper and the
sporting life of Joan Romney / P. G. Wodehouse.
p. cm.
ISBN 978-0-9801532-0-0 (Pbk)
1. Humorous stories, English. 2. England—Fiction. 3. Single men—
Fiction. 4. Single women—Fiction. 5. Short stories, English. I. Title.

PR6045.O53 Re 2013
823.9'12—dc23   2013953526

Printed in the United States of America
www.rushwaterpress.com
10 9 8 7 6 5 4 3 2 1

First Edition

Cover illustration: *Serious Business*, by Charles Dana Gibson (1905).

EDITORS' NOTE

These stories by P.G. Wodehouse, featuring his characters Reggie Pepper and Joan Romney, are collected here in book form for the first time. They originally appeared in magazines between 1905 and 1915. The text, edited by Patricia T. O'Conner and Stewart Kellerman for Rushwater Press, is published here under the title *Reggie and Joan: The Misadventures of Reggie Pepper* & *The Sporting Life of Joan Romney*.

CONTENTS

The Misadventures of Reggie Pepper

1	Absent Treatment	1
2	Helping Freddie	20
3	Disentangling Old Percy	40
4	Rallying Round Old George	64
5	Doing Clarence a Bit of Good	88
6	Concealed Art	109
7	The Test Case	130

The Sporting Life of Joan Romney

1	The Wire-Pullers	152
2	Petticoat Influence	166
3	Personally Conducted	184
4	Ladies and Gentlemen *v.* Players	200
5	Against the Clock	215

The Misadventures of Reggie Pepper

1. Absent Treatment

I WANT to tell you all about dear old Bobbie Cardew. It's a most interesting story. I can't put in any literary style and all that; but I don't have to, don't you know, because it goes on its Moral Lesson. If you're a man you mustn't miss it, because it'll be a warning to you; and if you're a woman you won't want to, because it's all about how a girl made a man feel pretty well fed up with things.

If you're a recent acquaintance of Bobbie's, you'll probably be surprised to hear that there was a time when he was more remarkable for the weakness of his memory than anything else. Dozens of fellows, who have only met Bobbie since the change took place, have been surprised when I told them that. Yet it's true. Believe *me*.

In the days when I first knew him Bobbie Cardew was about the most pronounced young rotter inside the four-mile radius. People have called me a silly ass, but I was never in the same class with Bobbie. When it came to being a silly ass, he was a plus four man, while my handicap was about six. Why, if I wanted him to dine with me, I used to post him a letter at the beginning of the week, and then the day before send him a telegram and a 'phone-call on the day itself, and—half an hour before the time we'd fixed—a messenger in a taxi, whose business it was to see that he got in and that the chauffeur had the address all correct. By doing that I generally managed to get him, unless he had left town before my messenger arrived.

The funny thing was that he wasn't altogether a fool in other ways. Deep down in him there was a kind of stratum of sense. I had known him, once or twice, show an almost human intelligence. But to reach that stratum, mind you, you needed dynamite.

At least, that's what I thought. But there was another way which hadn't occurred to me. Marriage, I mean. Marriage, the dynamite of the soul; that was what hit Bobbie. He married. Have you ever seen a bull-pup chasing a bee? The pup sees the bee. It looks good to him. But he doesn't know what's at the end of it till he gets there. It was like that with Bobbie. He fell in love, got married—with a sort of whoop, as if it were the greatest fun in the world—and then began to find out things.

She wasn't the sort of girl you would have expected Bobbie to rave about. And yet, I don't know. What I mean is, she worked for her living; and to a fellow who has never done a hand's turn in his life there's undoubtedly a sort of fascination, a kind of romance, about a girl who works for her living.

Her name was Anthony. Mary Anthony. She was about five feet six; she had a ton and a half of red-gold hair, grey eyes, and one of those determined chins. She was a hospital nurse. When Bobbie smashed himself up at polo, she was told off by the authorities to smooth his brow and rally round with cooling unguents and all that; and the old boy hadn't been up and about again for more than a week before they popped off to the registrar's and fixed it up. Quite the romance.

Bobbie broke the news to me at the club one evening, and next day he introduced me to her. I admired her. I've never worked myself—my name's Pepper, by the way. Almost forgot to mention it. Reggie Pepper. My uncle Edward was Pepper, Wells, and Co., the colliery people. He left me a sizable chunk of bullion—I say I've never worked myself, but I admire anyone who earns a living under difficulties, especially a girl. And this girl had had a rather unusually tough time of it, being an orphan and all that, and having had to do everything off her own bat for years.

Mary and I got along together splendidly. We don't now, but we'll come to that later. I'm speaking of the past. She seemed to think Bobbie the greatest thing on earth, judging by the way she looked at him when she thought I wasn't noticing. And Bobbie seemed to think the same about her. So that I came to the conclusion that, if only dear old Bobbie didn't forget to go to the wedding, they had a sporting chance of being quite happy.

Well, let's brisk up a bit here, and jump a year. The story doesn't really start till then.

They took a flat and settled down. I was in and out of the place quite a good deal. I kept my eyes open, and everything seemed to me to be running along as smooth as you could want. If this was marriage, I thought, I couldn't see why fellows were so frightened of it. There were a lot of worse things that could happen to a man.

But we now come to the incident of the Quiet Dinner, and it's just here that love's young dream hits a snag, and things begin to occur.

I happened to meet Bobbie in Piccadilly, and he asked me to come back to dinner at the flat. And, like a fool, instead of bolting and putting myself under police protection, I went.

When we got to the flat, there was Mrs. Bobbie looking—well, I tell you, it staggered me. Her gold hair was all piled up in waves and crinkles and things, with a what-d'-you-call-it of diamonds in it. And she was wearing the most perfectly ripping dress. I couldn't begin to describe it. I can only say it was the limit. It struck me that if this was how she was in the habit of looking every night when they were dining quietly at home together, it was no wonder that Bobbie liked domesticity.

"Here's old Reggie, dear," said Bobbie. "I've brought him home to have a bit of dinner. I'll 'phone down to the kitchen and ask them to send it up now—what?"

She stared at him as if she had never seen him before. Then she turned scarlet. Then she turned as white as a sheet. Then she gave a little laugh. It was most interesting to watch. Made me wish I was up a tree about eight hundred miles away. Then she recovered herself.

"I am so glad you were able to come, Mr. Pepper," she said, smiling at me.

And after that she was all right. At least, you would have said so. She talked a lot at dinner, and chaffed Bobbie, and played us rag-time on the piano afterwards, as if she hadn't a care in the world. Quite a jolly little party it was—not. I'm no lynx-eyed sleuth, and all that sort of thing, but I had seen her face at the beginning, and I knew that she was working the whole time, and working hard, to keep herself in hand, and that she would have given that diamond what's-its-name in her hair and everything else she possessed to have one good scream—just one. I've sat through some pretty thick evenings in my time, but that one had the rest beaten in a canter. At the very earliest moment I grabbed my hat and got away.

Having seen what I did, I wasn't particularly surprised to meet Bobbie at the club next day looking about as merry and bright as a lonely gum-drop at an Eskimo tea-party.

He started in straightaway. He seemed glad to have someone to talk to about it.

"Do you know how long I've been married?" he said.

I didn't exactly.

"About a year, isn't it?"

"Not *about* a year," he said, sadly. "Exactly a year—yesterday!"

Then I understood. I saw light—a regular flash of light.

"Yesterday was—?"

"The anniversary of the wedding. I'd arranged to take Mary to the Savoy, and on to Covent Garden. She particularly wanted to hear Caruso. I had the ticket for the box in my pocket. Do you know, all through dinner I had a kind of rummy idea that there was something I'd forgotten, but I couldn't think what?"

"Till your wife mentioned it?"

He nodded.

"She—mentioned it," he said, thoughtfully.

I didn't ask for details. Women with hair and chins like Mary's may be angels most of the time, but, when they take off their wings for a bit, they aren't half-hearted about it.

"To be absolutely frank, old top," said poor old Bobbie, in a broken sort of way, "my stock's pretty low at home."

There didn't seem much to be done. I just lit a cigarette and sat there. He didn't want to talk. Presently he went out. I stood at the window of our upper smoking-room, which looks out on to Piccadilly, and watched him. He walked slowly along for a few yards, stopped, then walked on again, and finally turned into a jeweller's. Which was an instance of what I meant when I said that deep down in him there was a certain stratum of sense.

It was from now on that I began to be really interested in this problem of Bobbie's married life. Of course, one's always mildly interested in one's friends' marriages, hoping they'll turn out well and all that; but this was different. The average man isn't like Bobbie, and the average girl isn't like Mary. It was that old business of the immovable mass and the irresistible force. There was Bobbie, ambling gently through life, a dear old chap in a hundred ways, but undoubtedly a chump of the first water.

And there was Mary, determined that he shouldn't be a chump. And Nature, mind you, on Bobbie's side. When Nature makes a chump like dear old Bobbie, she's proud of him, and doesn't want her handiwork disturbed. She gives him a sort of natural armour to protect him against outside interference. And that armour is shortness of memory. Shortness of memory keeps a man a chump, when, but for it, he might cease to be one. Take my case, for instance. I'm a chump. Well, if I had remembered half the things people have tried to teach me during my life, my size in hats would be about number nine. But I didn't. I forgot them. And it was just the same with Bobbie.

For about a week, perhaps a bit more, the recollection of that quiet little domestic evening bucked him up like a tonic. Elephants, I read somewhere, are champions at the memory business, but they were fools to Bobbie during that week. But bless you, the shock wasn't nearly big enough. It had dinted the armour, but it hadn't made a hole in it. Pretty soon he was back at the old game.

It was pathetic, don't you know. The poor girl loved him, and she was frightened. It was the thin end of the wedge, you see, and she knew it. A man who forgets what day he was married, when he's been married one year, will forget, at about the end of the fourth, that he's married at all. If she meant to get him in hand at all, she had got to do it now, before he began to drift away.

I saw that clearly enough, and I tried to make Bobbie see it, when he was by way of pouring out his troubles to me one afternoon. I can't remember what it was that he had forgotten the day before, but it was something she had asked him to bring home for her—it may have been a book.

"It's such a little thing to make a fuss about," said Bobbie. "And she knows that it's simply because I've got such an infernal memory about everything. I can't remember anything. Never could."

He talked on for a while, and, just as he was going, he pulled out a couple of sovereigns.

"Oh, by the way," he said.

"What's this for?" I asked, though I knew.

"I owe it you."

"How's that?" I said.

"Why, that bet on Tuesday. In the billiard-room. Murray and Brown were playing a hundred up, and I gave you two to one that Brown would win, and Murray beat him by twenty odd."

"So you do remember some things?" I said.

He got quite excited. Said that if I thought he was the sort of rotter who forgot to pay when he lost a bet, it was pretty rotten of me after knowing him all these years, and a lot more like that.

"Subside, laddie," I said.

Then I spoke to him like a father.

"What you've got to do, my old college chum," I said,

"is to pull yourself together, and jolly quick, too. As things are shaping, you're due for a nasty knock before you know what's hit you. You've got to make an effort. Don't say you can't. This two quid business shows that, even if your memory is rocky, you can remember some things. What you've got to do is to see that wedding anniversaries and so on are included in the list. It may be a brain-strain, but you can't get out of it."

"I suppose you're right," said Bobbie. "But it beats me why she thinks such a lot of these rotten little dates. What's it matter if I forget what day we were married on or what day she was born on or what day the cat had the measles? She knows I love her just as much as if I were a memorizing freak at the halls."

"That's not enough for a woman," I said. "They want to be shown. Bear that in mind, and you're all right. Forget it, and there'll be trouble."

He chewed the knob of his stick.

"Women are frightfully rummy," he said, gloomily.

"You should have thought of that before you married one," I said.

I don't see that I could have done any more. I had put the whole thing in a nutshell for him. You would have thought he'd have seen the point, and that it would have made him brace up and get a hold on himself. But, no. Off he went again in the same old way. I gave up arguing with him. I had a good deal of time on my hands, but not enough to amount to anything when it was a question of reforming dear old Bobbie by argument. If you see a man asking for trouble, and insisting on getting it, the only thing to do is to stand by and wait till it comes to him. After that you may get a chance. But till then there's nothing to be done. But I thought a lot about him.

Bobbie didn't get into the soup all at once. Weeks went by, and months, and still nothing happened. Now and then he'd come into the club with a kind of cloud on his shining morning face, and I'd know that there had been doings in the home; but it wasn't till well on in the spring that he got the thunderbolt just where he had been asking for it—in the thorax.

I was smoking a quiet cigarette one morning in the window looking out over Piccadilly, and watching the buses and motors going up one way and down the other—most interesting it is; I often do it—when in rushed Bobbie, with his eyes bulging and his face the colour of an oyster, waving a piece of paper in his hand.

"Reggie," he said. "Reggie, old top, she's gone!"

"Gone!" I said. "Who?"

"Mary, of course! Gone! Left me! Gone!"

"Where?" I said.

Silly question? Perhaps you're right. Anyhow, dear old Bobbie nearly foamed at the mouth.

"Where? How should I know where? Here, read this."

He pushed the paper into my hand. It was a letter.

"Go on," said Bobbie. "Read it."

So I did. It certainly was quite a letter. There was not much of it, but it was all to the point.

This is what it said:

"My dear Bobbie, I am going away. When you care enough about me to remember to wish me many happy returns on my birthday, I will come back. My address will be Box 341, *London Morning News*."

I read it twice, then I said, "Well, why don't you?"

"Why don't I what?"

"Why don't you wish her many happy returns? It doesn't seem much to ask."

"But she says on her birthday."

"Well, when is her birthday?"

"Can't you understand?" said Bobbie. "I've forgotten."

"Forgotten!" I said.

"Yes," said Bobbie. "Forgotten."

"How do you mean, forgotten?" I said. "Forgotten whether it's the twentieth or the twenty-first, or what? How near do you get to it?"

"I know it came somewhere between the first of January and the thirty-first of December. That's how near I get to it."

"Think."

"Think? What's the use of saying 'Think'? Think I haven't thought? I've been knocking sparks out of my brain ever since I opened that letter."

"And you can't remember?"

"No."

I rang the bell and ordered restoratives.

"Well, Bobbie," I said, "it's a pretty hard case to spring on an untrained amateur like me. Suppose someone had come to Sherlock Holmes and said, 'Mr. Holmes, here's a case for you. When is my wife's birthday?' Wouldn't that have given Sherlock a jolt? However, I know enough about the game to understand that a fellow can't shoot off his deductive theories unless you start him with a clue, so rouse yourself out of that pop-eyed trance and come across with two or three. For instance, can't you remember the last time she had a birthday? What sort of weather was it? That might fix the month."

Bobbie shook his head.

"It was just ordinary weather, as near as I can recollect."

"Warm?"

"Warmish."

"Or cold?"

"Well, fairly cold, perhaps. I can't remember."

I ordered two more of the same. They seemed indicated in the Young Detective's Manual. "You're a great help, Bobbie," I said. "An invaluable assistant. Once of those indispensable adjuncts without which no home is complete."

Bobbie seemed to be thinking.

"I've got it," he said suddenly. "Look here. I gave her a present on her last birthday. All we have to do is to go to the shop, hunt up the date when it was bought, and the thing's done."

"Absolutely. What did you give her?"

He sagged.

"I can't remember," he said.

Getting ideas is like golf. Some days you are right off it, others it's as easy as falling off a log. I don't suppose dear old Bobbie had ever had two ideas in the same morning before in his life; but now he did it without an effort. He just loosed another dry Martini into the undergrowth, and before you could turn round it had flushed quite a brain-wave.

Do you know those little books called "When were you born?" There's one for each month. They tell you your character, your talents, your strong points, and your weak points at fourpence half-penny a go. Bobbie's idea was to buy the whole twelve, and go through them till we found out which month hit off Mary's character. That would give us the month, and narrow it down a whole lot.

A pretty hot idea for a non-thinker like dear old Bobbie. We sallied out at once. He took half and I took half, and we settled down to work. As I say, it sounded good. But when we came to go into the thing, we saw that there was a flaw. There was plenty of information all right, but there wasn't a single month that didn't have something that exactly hit off Mary. For instance, in the December book it said, "December people are apt to keep their own secrets. They are extensive travelers." Well, Mary had certainly kept her secret, and she had travelled quite extensively enough for Bobbie's needs. Then, October people were "born with original ideas" and "loved moving." You couldn't have summed up Mary's little jaunt more neatly. February people had "wonderful memories"—Mary's speciality.

We took a bit of a rest, then had another go at the thing.

Bobbie was all for May, because the book said that women born in that month were "inclined to be capricious, which is always a barrier to a happy married life"; but I plumped for February, because February women "are unusually determined to have their own way, are very earnest, and expect a full return in their companions or mates." Which he owned was about as like Mary as anything could be.

In the end he tore the books up, stamped on them, burnt them, and went home.

It was wonderful what a change the next few days made in dear old Bobbie. Have you ever seen that picture, "The Soul's Awakening"? It represents a flapper of sorts gazing in a startled sort of way into the middle distance with a look in her eyes that seems to say, "Surely that is George's step I hear on the mat! Can this be love?" Well, Bobbie had a soul's awakening too. I don't suppose he had ever troubled to think in his life before—not really *think*. But now he was wearing his brain to the bone. It was painful in a way, of course, to see a fellow human being so thoroughly in the soup, but I felt strongly that it was all for the best. I could see as plainly as possible that all these brain-storms were improving Bobbie out of knowledge. When it was all over he might possibly become a rotter again of a sort, but it would only be a pale reflection of the rotter he had been. It bore out the idea I had always had that what he needed was a real good jolt.

I saw a great deal of him these days. I was his best friend, and he came to me for sympathy. I gave it him, too, with both hands, but I never failed to hand him the Moral Lesson when I had him weak.

One day he came to me as I was sitting in the club, and I could see that he had had an idea. He looked happier than he had done in weeks.

"Reggie," he said, "I'm on the trail. This time I'm convinced that I shall pull it off. I've remembered something of vital importance."

"Yes?" I said.

"I remember distinctly," he said, "that on Mary's last birthday we went together to the Coliseum. How does that hit you?"

"It's a fine bit of memorizing," I said; "but how does it help?"

"Why, they change the programme every week there."

"Ah!" I said. "Now you are talking."

"And the week we went one of the turns was Professor Someone's Terpsichorean Cats. I recollect them distinctly. Now, are we narrowing it down, or aren't we? Reggie, I'm going round to the Coliseum this minute, and I'm going to dig the date of those Terpsichorean Cats out of them, if I have to use a crowbar."

So that got him within six days; for the management treated us like brothers; brought out the archives, and ran agile fingers over the pages till they treed the cats in the middle of May.

"I told you it was May," said Bobbie. "Maybe you'll listen to me another time."

"If you've any sense," I said, "there won't be another time."

And Bobbie said that there wouldn't.

Once you get your memory on the run, it parts as if it enjoyed doing it. I had just got off to sleep that night when my telephone bell rang. It was Bobbie, of course.

He didn't apologize.

"Reggie," he said, "I've got it now for certain. It's just come to me. We saw those Terpsichorean Cats at a *matinée*, old man."

"Yes?" I said.

"Well, don't you see that that brings it down to two days? It must have been either Wednesday the seventh or Saturday the tenth."

"Yes," I said, "if they didn't have daily *matinées* at the Coliseum."

I heard him give a sort of howl.

"Bobbie," I said. My feet were freezing, but I was fond of him.

"Well?"

"I've remembered something too. It's this. The day you went to the Coliseum I lunched with you both at the Ritz. You had forgotten to bring any money with you, so you wrote a cheque."

"But I'm always writing cheques."

"You are. But this was for a tenner, and made out to the hotel. Hunt up your cheque-book and see how many cheques for ten pounds payable to the Ritz Hotel you wrote out between May the fifth and May the tenth."

He gave a kind of gulp.

"Reggie," he said, "you're a genius. I've always said so. I believe you've got it. Hold the line."

Presently he came back again. "Halloa!" he said.

"I'm here," I said.

"It was the eighth. Reggie, old man, I—"

"Topping," I said. "Good night."

It was working along into the small hours now, but I thought I might as well make a night of it and finish the thing up, so I rang up an hotel near the Strand.

"Put me through to Mrs. Cardew," I said.

"It's late," said the man at the other end.

"And getting later every minute," I said. "Buck along, laddie."

I waited patiently. I had missed my beauty-sleep, and my feet had frozen hard, but I was past regrets.

"What is the matter?" said Mary's voice.

"My feet are cold," I said. "But I didn't call you up to tell you that particularly. I've just been chatting with Bobbie, Mrs. Cardew."

"Oh! Is that Mr. Pepper?"

"Yes. He's remembered it, Mrs. Cardew."

She gave a sort of scream. I've often thought how interesting it must be to be one of those Exchange girls. The things they must hear, don't you know. Bobbie's howl and gulp and Mrs. Bobbie's scream and all about my feet and all that. Most interesting it must be.

"He's remembered it!" she gasped. "Did you tell him?"

"No."

Well, I hadn't.

"Mr. Pepper."

"Yes?"

"Was he—has he been—was he very worried?"

I chuckled. This was where I was billed to be the life and soul of the party.

"Worried! He was about the most worried man between here and Edinburgh. He has been worrying as if he was paid to do it by the nation. He has started out to worry after breakfast, and—"

Oh, well, you can never tell with women. My idea was that we should pass the rest of the night slapping each other on the back across the wire, and telling each other what bally brainy conspirators we were, don't you know, and all that. But I'd got just as far as this, when she bit at me. Absolutely! I heard the snap. And then she said "Oh!" in that choked kind of way. And when a woman says "Oh!" like that, it means all the bad words she'd love to say if she only knew them.

And then she began.

"What brutes men are! What horrid brutes! How you could stand by and see poor dear Bobbie worrying himself into a fever, when a word from you would have put everything right, I can't—"

"But—"

"And you call yourself his friend! His friend!" (Metallic laugh, most unpleasant.) "It shows how one can be deceived. I used to think you a kind-hearted man."

"But, I say, when I suggested the thing, you thought it perfectly—"

"I thought it hateful, abominable."

"But you said it was absolutely top—"

"I said nothing of the kind. And if I did, I didn't mean it. I don't wish to be unjust, Mr. Pepper, but I must say that to me there seems to be something positively fiendish in a man who can go out of his way to separate a husband from his wife, simply in order to amuse himself by gloating over his agony—"

"But—!"

"When one single word would have—"

"But you made me promise not to—" I bleated.

"And if I did, do you suppose I didn't expect you to have the sense to break your promise?"

I had finished. I had no further observations to make. I hung up the receiver, and crawled into bed.

I still see Bobbie when he comes to the club, but I do not visit the old homestead. He is friendly, but he stops short of issuing invitations. I ran across Mary at the Academy last week, and her eyes went through me like a couple of bullets through a pat of butter. And as they came out of the other side, and I limped off to piece myself together again, there occurred to me the simple epitaph which, when I am no more, I intend to have inscribed on my tombstone. It was this: "He was a man who acted from the best motives. There is one born every minute."

—Strand, March 1911

2. Helping Freddie

I DON'T want to bore you, don't you know, and all that sort of rot, but I must tell you about dear old Freddie Meadowes. I'm not a flier at literary style, and all that, but I'll get some writer chappie to give the thing a wash and brush up when I've finished, so that'll be all right.

Dear old Freddie, don't you know, has been a dear old pal of mine for years and years; so when I went into the club one morning and found him sitting alone in a dark corner, staring glassily at nothing, and generally looking like the last rose of summer, you can understand I was quite disturbed about it. As a rule, the old rotter is the life and soul of our set. Quite the little lump of fun, and all that sort of thing.

Jimmy Pinkerton was with me at the time. Jimmy's a fellow who writes plays; a deuced brainy sort of fellow. My name's Pepper, by the way—Reggie Pepper. My uncle

Edward was Pepper, Wells and Co., the colliery people. When he died, he left me a pretty decent bit of money. Well, as I was saying, Jimmy was with me, and between us we set to work to question the poor pop-eyed chappie, until finally we got at what the matter was.

As we might have guessed, it was a girl. He had had a quarrel with Angela West, the girl he was engaged to, and she had broken off the engagement. What the row had been about he didn't say, but apparently she was pretty well fed up. She wouldn't let him come near her, refused to talk on the phone, and sent back his letters unopened.

I was sorry for poor old Freddie. I knew what it felt like. I was once in love myself with a girl called Elizabeth Shoolbred, and the fact that she couldn't stand me at any price will be recorded in my autobiography. I knew the thing for Freddie.

"Change of scene is what you want, old scout," I said. "Come with me to Marvis Bay. I've taken a cottage there. Jimmy's coming down on the twenty-fourth. We'll be a cosy party."

"He's absolutely right," said Jimmy. "Change of scene's the thing. I knew a man. Girl refused him. Man went abroad. Two months later girl wired him, 'Come back. Muriel.' Man started to write out a reply; suddenly found that he couldn't remember girl's surname; so never answered at all."

But Freddie wouldn't be comforted. He just went on looking as if he had swallowed his last sixpence. However, I got him to promise to come to Marvis Bay with me. He said he might as well be there as anywhere.

Do you know Marvis Bay? It's in Dorsetshire. It isn't what you'd call a fiercely exciting spot, but it has its good points. You spend the day there bathing and sitting on the sands, and in the evening you stroll out on the shore with the gnats. At nine o'clock you rub ointment on the wounds and go to bed.

It seemed to suit poor old Freddie. Once the moon was up and the breeze sighing in the trees, you couldn't drag him from that beach with a rope. He became quite a popular pet with the gnats. They'd hang round waiting for him to come out, and would give perfectly good strollers the miss-in-baulk just so as to be in good condition for him.

Yes, it was a peaceful sort of life, but by the end of the first week I began to wish that Jimmy Pinkerton had arranged to come down earlier: for as a companion Freddie, poor old chap, wasn't anything to write home to mother about. When he wasn't chewing a pipe and scowling at the carpet, he was sitting at the piano, playing "The Rosary" with one finger. He couldn't play anything except "The Rosary," and he couldn't play much of that. Somewhere round about the third bar a fuse would blow out, and he'd have to start all over again.

He was playing it as usual one morning when I came in from bathing.

"Reggie," he said, in a hollow voice, looking up, "I've seen her."

"Seen her?" I said. "What, Miss West?"

"I was down at the post office, getting the letters, and we met in the doorway. She cut me!"

He started "The Rosary" again, and side-slipped in the second bar.

"Reggie," he said, "you ought never to have brought me here. I must go away."

"Go away?" I said. "Don't talk such rot. This is the best thing that could have happened. This is where you come out strong."

"She cut me."

"Never mind. Be a sportsman. Have another dash at her."

"She looked clean through me!"

"Of course she did. But don't mind that. Put this thing in my hands. I'll see you through. Now, what you want," I said, "is to place her under some obligation to you. What you want is to get her timidly thanking you. What you want—"

"But what's she going to thank me timidly for?"

I thought for a moment.

"Look out for a chance and save her from drowning," I said.

"I can't swim," said Freddie.

That was Freddie all over, don't you know. A dear old chap in a thousand ways, but no help to a fellow, if you know what I mean.

He cranked up the piano once more and I sprinted for the open.

I strolled out on to the sands and began to think this thing over. There was no doubt that the brain-work had got to be done by me. Dear old Freddie had his strong qualities. He was top-hole at polo, and in happier days

I've heard him give an imitation of cats fighting in a backyard that would have surprised you. But apart from that he wasn't a man of enterprise.

Well, don't you know, I was rounding some rocks, with my brain whirring like a dynamo, when I caught sight of a blue dress, and, by Jove, it was the girl. I had never met her, but Freddie had sixteen photographs of her sprinkled round his bedroom, and I knew I couldn't be mistaken. She was sitting on the sand, helping a small, fat child build a castle. On a chair close by was an elderly lady reading a novel. I heard the girl call her "aunt." So, doing the Sherlock Holmes business, I deduced that the fat child was her cousin. It struck me that if Freddie had been there he would probably have tried to work up some sentiment about the kid on the strength of it. Personally I couldn't manage it. I don't think I ever saw a child who made me feel less sentimental. He was one of those round, bulging kids.

After he had finished the castle he seemed to get bored with life, and began to whimper. The girl took him off to where a fellow was selling sweets at a stall. And I walked on.

Now, fellows, if you ask them, will tell you that I'm a chump. Well, I don't mind. I admit it. I *am* a chump. All the Peppers have been chumps. But what I do say is that every now and then, when you'd least expect it, I get a pretty hot brain-wave; and that's what happened now. I doubt if the idea that came to me then would have occurred to a single one of any dozen of the brainiest chappies you care to name.

It came to me on my return journey. I was walking back along the shore, when I saw the fat kid meditatively smacking a jelly-fish with a spade. The girl wasn't with him. In fact, there didn't seem to be any one in sight. I was just going to pass on when I got the brain-wave. I thought the whole thing out in a flash, don't you know. From what I had seen of the two, the girl was evidently fond of this kid, and, anyhow, he was her cousin, so what I said to myself was this: If I kidnap this young heavy-weight for the moment, and if, when the girl has got frightfully anxious about where he can have got to, dear old Freddie suddenly appears leading the infant by the hand and telling a story to the effect that he has found him wandering at large about the country and practically saved his life, why, the girl's gratitude is bound to make her chuck hostilities and be friends again. So I gathered in the kid and made off with him. All the way home I pictured that scene of reconciliation. I could see it so vividly, don't you know, that, by George, it gave me quite a choky feeling in my throat.

Freddie, dear old chap, was rather slow at getting on to the fine points of the idea. When I appeared, carrying the kid, and dumped him down in our sitting-room, he didn't absolutely effervesce with joy, if you know what I mean. The kid had started to bellow by this time, and poor old Freddie seemed to find it rather trying.

"Stop it!" he said. "Do you think nobody's got any troubles except you? What the deuce is all this, Reggie?"

The kid came back at him with a yell that made the window rattle. I raced to the kitchen and fetched a jar of honey. It was the right stuff. The kid stopped bellowing and began to smear his face with the stuff.

"Well?" said Freddie, when silence had set in. I explained the idea. After a while it began to strike him.

"You're not such a fool as you look, sometimes, Reggie," he said handsomely. "I'm bound to say this seems pretty good."

And he disentangled the kid from the honey-jar and took him out, to scour the beach for Angela.

I don't know when I've felt so happy. I was so fond of dear old Freddie that to know that he was soon going to be his old bright self again made me feel as if somebody had left me about a million pounds. I was leaning back in a chair on the veranda, smoking peacefully, when down the road I saw the old boy returning, and, by George, the kid was still with him. And Freddie looked as if he hadn't a friend in the world.

"Hello!" I said. "Couldn't you find her?"

"Yes, I found her," he replied, with one of those bitter, hollow laughs.

"Well, then—?"

Freddie sank into a chair and groaned.

"This isn't her cousin, you idiot!" he said. "He's no relation at all. He's just a kid she happened to meet on the beach. She had never seen him before in her life."

"What! Who is he, then?"

"I don't know. Oh, Lord, I've had a time! Thank goodness you'll probably spend the next few years of your life in Dartmoor for kidnapping. That's my only consolation. I'll come and jeer at you through the bars."

"Tell me all, old boy," I said.

It took him a good long time to tell the story, for he broke off in the middle of nearly every sentence to call me names, but I gathered gradually what had happened. She had listened like an iceberg while he told the story he had prepared, and then—well, she didn't actually call him a liar, but she gave him to understand in a general sort of way that if he and Dr. Cook ever happened to meet, and started swapping stories, it would be about the biggest duel on record. And then he had crawled away with the kid, licked to a splinter.

"And mind, this is your affair," he concluded. "I'm not mixed up in it at all. If you want to escape your sentence, you'd better go and find the kid's parents and return him before the police come for you."

By Jove, you know, till I started to tramp the place with this infernal kid, I never had a notion it would have been so deuced difficult to restore a child to its anxious parents. It's a mystery to me how kidnappers ever get caught. I searched Marvis Bay like a bloodhound, but nobody came forward to claim the infant. You'd have thought, from the lack of interest in him, that he was stopping there all by himself in a cottage of his own. It wasn't till, by an inspiration, I thought to ask the sweet-stall man that I found out that his name was Medwin, and that his parents lived at a place called Ocean Rest, in Beach Road.

I shot off there like an arrow and knocked at the door. Nobody answered. I knocked again. I could hear movements inside, but nobody came. I was just going to get to work on that knocker in such a way that the idea would filter through into these people's heads that I wasn't standing there just for the fun of the thing, when a voice from somewhere above shouted, "Hi!"

I looked up and saw a round, pink face, with grey whiskers east and west of it, staring down from an upper window.

"Hi!" it shouted again.

"What the deuce do you mean by 'Hi'?" I said.

"You can't come in," said the face. "Hello, is that Tootles?"

"My name is not Tootles, and I don't want to come in," I said. "Are you Mr. Medwin? I've brought back your son."

"I see him. Peep-bo, Tootles! Dadda can see 'oo!"

The face disappeared with a jerk. I could hear voices. The face reappeared.

"Hi!"

I churned the gravel madly.

"Do you live here?" said the face.

"I'm staying here for a few weeks."

"What's your name?"

"Pepper. But—"

"Pepper? Any relation to Edward Pepper, the colliery owner?"

"My uncle. But—"

"I used to know him well. Dear old Edward Pepper! I wish I was with him now."

"I wish you were," I said.

He beamed down at me.

"This is most fortunate," he said. "We were wondering what we were to do with Tootles. You see, we have the mumps here. My daughter Bootles has just developed mumps. Tootles must not be exposed to the risk of infection. We could not think what we were to do with him. It was most fortunate your finding him. He strayed from his nurse. I would hesitate to trust him to the care of a stranger, but you are different. Any nephew of Edward Pepper's has my implicit confidence. You must take Tootles to your house. It will be an ideal arrangement. I have written to my brother in London to come and fetch him. He may be here in a few days."

"May!"

"He is a busy man, of course; but he should certainly be here within a week. Till then Tootles can stop with you. It is an excellent plan. Very much obliged to you. Your wife will like Tootles."

"I haven't got a wife," I yelled; but the window had closed with a bang, as if the man with the whiskers had found a germ trying to escape, don't you know, and had headed it off just in time.

I breathed a deep breath and wiped my forehead.

The window flew up again.

"Hi!"

A package weighing about a ton hit me on the head and burst like a bomb.

"Did you catch it?" said the face, reappearing. "Dear me, you missed it! Never mind. You can get it at the grocer's. Ask for Bailey's Granulated Breakfast Chips. Tootles takes them for breakfast with a little milk. Be certain to get Bailey's."

My spirit was broken, if you know what I mean. I accepted the situation. Taking Tootles by the hand, I walked slowly away. Napoleon's retreat from Moscow was a picnic by the side of it.

As we turned up the road we met Freddie's Angela.

The sight of her had a marked effect on the kid Tootles. He pointed at her and said, "Wah!"

The girl stopped and smiled. I loosed the kid, and he ran to her.

"Well, baby?" she said, bending down to him. "So father found you again, did he? Your little son and I made friends on the beach this morning," she said to me.

This was the limit. Coming on top of that interview with the whiskered lunatic it so utterly unnerved me, don't you know, that she had nodded good-bye and was half-way down the road before I caught up with my breath enough to deny the charge of being the infant's father.

I hadn't expected dear old Freddie to sing with joy when he found out what had happened, but I did think he might have shown a little more manly fortitude. He leaped up, glared at the kid, and clutched his head. He didn't speak for a long time, but, on the other hand, when he began he did not leave off for a long time. He was quite emotional, dear old boy. It beat me where he could have picked up such expressions.

"Well," he said, when he had finished, "say something! Heavens! man, why don't you say something?"

"You don't give me a chance, old top," I said

soothingly.

"What are you going to do about it?"

"What *can* we do about it?"

"We can't spend our time acting as nurses to this—this exhibit."

He got up.

"I'm going back to London," he said.

"Freddie!" I cried. "Freddie, old man!" My voice shook. "Would you desert a pal at a time like this?"

"I would. This is your business, and you've got to manage it."

"Freddie," I said, "you've got to stand by me. You must. Do you realize that this child has to be undressed, and bathed, and dressed again? You wouldn't leave me to do all that single-handed? Freddie, old scout, we were at school together. Your mother likes me. You owe me a tenner."

He sat down again.

"Oh, well," he said resignedly.

"Besides, old top," I said, "I did it all for your sake, don't you know?"

He looked at me in a curious way.

"Reggie," he said, in a strained voice, "one moment. I'll stand a good deal, but I won't stand for being expected to be grateful."

Looking back at it, I see that what saved me from Colney Hatch in that crisis was my bright idea of buying up most of the contents of the local sweet-shop. By serving out sweets to the kid practically incessantly we managed to get through the rest of that day pretty satisfactorily. At eight o'clock he fell asleep in a chair, and, having undressed him by unbuttoning every button in sight and, where there were no buttons, pulling till something gave, we carried him up to bed.

Freddie stood looking at the pile of clothes on the floor and I knew what he was thinking. To get the kid undressed had been simple—a mere matter of muscle. But how were we to get him into his clothes again? I stirred the pile with my foot. There was a long linen arrangement which might have been anything. Also a strip of pink flannel which was like nothing on earth. We looked at each other and smiled wanly.

But in the morning I remembered that there were children at the next bungalow but one. We went there before breakfast and borrowed their nurse. Women are wonderful, by George they are! She had that kid dressed and looking fit for anything in about eight minutes. I showered wealth on her, and she promised to come in morning and evening. I sat down to breakfast almost cheerful again. It was the first bit of silver lining there had been to the cloud up to date.

"And after all," I said, "there's lots to be said for having a child about the house, if you know what I mean. Kind of cosy and domestic—what!"

Just then the kid upset the milk over Freddie's trousers, and when he had come back after changing his clothes he began to talk about what a much-maligned man King Herod was. The more he saw of Tootles, he said, the less he wondered at those impulsive views of his on infanticide.

Two days later Jimmy Pinkerton came down. Jimmy took one look at the kid, who happened to be howling at the moment, and picked up his portmanteau.

"For me," he said, "the hotel. I can't write dialogue with that sort of thing going on. Whose work is this? Which of you adopted this little treasure?"

I told him about Mr. Medwin and the mumps. Jimmy seemed interested.

"I might work this up for the stage," he said. "It wouldn't make a bad situation for act two of a farce."

"Farce!" snarled poor old Freddie.

"Rather. Curtain of act one on hero, a well-meaning, half-baked sort of idiot just like—that is to say, a well-meaning, half-baked sort of idiot, kidnapping the child. Second act, his adventures with it. I'll rough it out to-night. Come along and show me the hotel, Reggie."

As we went I told him the rest of the story—the Angela part. He laid down his portmanteau and looked at me like an owl through his glasses.

"What!" he said. "Why, hang it, this *is* a play, ready-made. It's the old 'Tiny Hand' business. Always safe stuff. Parted lovers. Lisping child. Reconciliation over the little cradle. It's big. Child, centre. Girl L.C.; Freddie, up stage, by the piano. Can Freddie play the piano?"

"He can play a little of 'The Rosary' with one finger."

Jimmy shook his head.

"No; we shall have to cut out the soft music. But the rest's all right. Look here." He squatted in the sand. "This stone is the girl. This bit of seaweed's the child. This nutshell is Freddie. Dialogue leading up to child's line.

Child speaks like, 'Boofer lady, does 'oo love dadda?' Business of outstretched hands. Hold picture for a moment. Freddie crosses L., takes girl's hand. Business of swallowing lump in throat. Then big speech. 'Ah, Marie,' or whatever her name is—Jane—Agnes—Angela? Very well. 'Ah, Angela, has not this gone on too long? A little child rebukes us! Angela!' And so on. Freddie must work up his own part. I'm just giving you the general outline. And we must get a good line for the child. 'Boofer lady, does 'oo love dadda?' isn't definite enough. We want something more—ah! 'Kiss Freddie,' that's it. Short, crisp, and has the punch."

"But, Jimmy, old top," I said, "the only objection is, don't you know, that there's no way of getting the girl to the cottage. She cuts Freddie. She wouldn't come within a mile of him."

Jimmy frowned.

"That's awkward," he said. "Well, we shall have to make it an exterior set instead of an interior. We can easily corner her on the beach somewhere, when we're ready. Meanwhile, we must get the kid letter-perfect. First rehearsal for lines and business eleven sharp to-morrow."

Poor old Freddie was in such a gloomy state of mind that we decided not to tell him the idea till we had finished coaching the kid. He wasn't in the mood to have a thing like that hanging over him. So we concentrated on Tootles. And pretty early in the proceedings we saw that the only way to get Tootles worked up to the spirit of the thing was to introduce sweets of some sort as a sub-motive, so to speak.

"The chief difficulty," said Jimmy Pinkerton at the end of the first rehearsal, "is to establish a connection in the kid's mind between his line and the sweets. Once he has grasped the basic fact that those two words, clearly spoken, result automatically in acid-drops, we have got a success."

I've often thought, don't you know, how interesting it must be to be one of those animal-trainer Johnnies: to stimulate the dawning intelligence, and that sort of thing. Well, this was every bit as exciting. Some days success seemed to be staring us in the eye, and the kid got the line out as if he'd been an old professional. And then he'd go all to pieces again. And time was flying.

"We must hurry up, Jimmy," I said. "The kid's uncle may arrive any day now and take him away."

"And we haven't an understudy," said Jimmy. "There's something in that. We must work! My goodness, that kid's a bad study. I've known deaf-mutes who would have learned the part quicker."

I will say this for the kid, though: he was a trier. Failure didn't discourage him. Whenever there was any kind of sweet near he had a dash at his line, and kept on saying something till he got what he was after. His only fault was his uncertainty. Personally, I would have been prepared to risk it, and start the performance at the first opportunity, but Jimmy said no.

"We're not nearly ready," said Jimmy. "To-day, for instance, he said 'Kick Freddie.' That's not going to win any girl's heart. And she might do it, too. No; we must postpone production awhile yet."

But, by George, we didn't. The curtain went up the very next afternoon.

It was nobody's fault—certainly not mine. It was just Fate. Freddie had settled down at the piano, and I was leading the kid out of the house to exercise it, when, just as we'd got out to the veranda, along came the girl Angela on her way to the beach. The kid set up his usual yell at the sight of her, and she stopped at the foot of the steps.

"Hello, baby!" she said. "Good morning," she said to me. "May I come up?"

She didn't wait for an answer. She just came. She seemed to be that sort of girl. She came up on the veranda and started fussing over the kid. And six feet away, mind you, Freddie smiting the piano in the sitting-room. It was a dashed disturbing situation, don't you know. At any minute Freddie might take it into his head to come out on to the veranda, and we hadn't even begun to rehearse him in his part.

I tried to break up the scene.

"We were just going down to the beach," I said.

"Yes?" said the girl. She listened for a moment. "So you're having your piano tuned?" she said. "My aunt has been trying to find a tuner for ours. Do you mind if I go in and tell this man to come on to us when he's finished here?"

"Er—not yet!" I said. "Not yet, if you don't mind. He can't bear to be disturbed when he's working. It's the artistic temperament. I'll tell him later."

"Very well," she said, getting up to go. "Ask him to call at Pine Bungalow. West is the name. Oh, he seems to have stopped. I suppose he will be out in a minute now. I'll wait."

"Don't you think—shouldn't we be going on to the beach?" I said.

She had started talking to the kid and didn't hear. She was feeling in her pocket for something.

"The beach," I babbled.

"See what I've brought for you, baby," she said. And, by George, don't you know, she held up in front of the kid's bulging eyes a chunk of toffee about the size of the Automobile Club.

That finished it. We had just been having a long rehearsal, and the kid was all worked up in his part. He got it right first time.

"Kiss Fweddie!" he shouted.

And the front door opened, and Freddie came out on to the veranda, for all the world as if he had been taking a cue.

He looked at the girl, and the girl looked at him. I looked at the ground, and the kid looked at the toffee.

"Kiss Fweddie!" he yelled. "Kiss Fweddie!"

The girl was still holding up the toffee, and the kid did what Jimmy Pinkerton would have called "business of outstretched hands" towards it.

"Kiss Fweddie!" he shrieked.

"What does this mean?" said the girl, turning to me.

"You'd better give it to him, don't you know," I said. "He'll go on till you do."

She gave the kid his toffee, and he subsided. Poor old Freddie still stood there gaping, without a word.

"What does it mean?" said the girl again. Her face was pink, and her eyes were sparkling in the sort of way, don't you know, that makes a fellow feel as if he hadn't any bones in him, if you know what I mean. Did you ever tread on your partner's dress at a dance and tear it, and see her smile at you like an angel and say: *"Please* don't apologize. It's nothing," and then suddenly meet her clear blue eyes and feel as if you had stepped on the teeth of a rake and had the handle jump up and hit you in the face? Well, that's how Freddie's Angela looked.

"Well?" she said, and her teeth gave a little click.

I gulped. Then I said it was nothing. Then I said it was nothing much. Then I said, "Oh, well, it was this way." And, after a few brief remarks about Jimmy Pinkerton, I told her all about it. And all the while Idiot Freddie stood there gaping, without a word.

And the girl didn't speak, either. She just stood listening.

And then she began to laugh. I never heard a girl laugh so much. She leaned against the side of the veranda and shrieked. And all the while Freddie, the World's Champion Chump, stood there, saying nothing.

Well I sidled towards the steps. I had said all I had to say, and it seemed to me that about here the stage-direction "exit" was written in my part. I gave poor old Freddie up in despair. If only he had said a word, it might have been all right. But there he stood, speechless. What can a fellow do with a fellow like that?

Just out of sight of the house I met Jimmy Pinkerton.

"Hello, Reggie!" he said. "I was just coming to you.

Where's the kid? We must have a big rehearsal to-day."

"No good," I said sadly. "It's all over. The thing's finished. Poor dear old Freddie has made an ass of himself and killed the whole show."

"Tell me," said Jimmy.

I told him.

"Fluffed in his lines, did he?" said Jimmy, nodding thoughtfully. "It's always the way with these amateurs. We must go back at once. Things look bad, but it may not be too late," he said as we started. "Even now a few well-chosen words from a man of the world, and—"

"Great Scott!" I cried. "Look!"

In front of the cottage stood six children, a nurse, and the fellow from the grocer's staring. From the windows of the houses opposite projected about four hundred heads of both sexes, staring. Down the road came galloping five more children, a dog, three men, and a boy, about to stare. And on our porch, as unconscious of the spectators as if they had been alone in the Sahara, stood Freddie and Angela, clasped in each other's arms.

Dear old Freddie may have been fluffy in his lines, but, by George, his business had certainly gone with a bang!

—Strand, September 1911

3. Disentangling Old Percy

DOESN'T some poet or philosopher fellow say that it's when our intentions are best that we always make the most poisonous bloomers? I can't put my hand on the passage, but you'll find it in Shakespeare or somewhere, I'm pretty certain. Anyhow, it's always that way with me.

And the affair of Percy Craye is a case in point.

I had dined with Percy (a dear old pal of mine) one night at the Bank of England—he's in the Guards, and it was his turn to be on hand there and prevent any blighter trying to slide in and help himself—and as he was seeing me out he said, "Reggie, old top" (my name's Reggie Pepper)—"Reggie, old top, I'm rather worried."

"Are you, Percy, old pal?" I said.

"Yes, Reggie, old fellow," he said, "I am. It's like this. The Booles have asked me down to their place for the week-end, and I don't know whether to go or not. You see, they have family prayers at half-past eight sharp, and besides that there's a frightful risk of music after dinner. On the other hand, young Roderick Boole thinks he can play piquet."

"I should go," I said.

"But I'm not sure Roderick's going to be there this time."

It was a pretty tricky problem, and I didn't wonder poor old Percy had looked pale and fagged at dinner.

Then I had the idea which really started all the trouble.

"Why don't you consult a palmist?" I said.

"That's not a bad idea," said Percy.

"Go and see Dorothea in Bond Street. She's a wonder. She'll settle it for you in a second. She'll see from your lines that you are thinking of making a journey, and she'll either tell you to fizz ahead, which will mean that Roderick will be there, or else to keep away because she sees disaster."

"You seem well up in this sort of thing."

"I've been to a good many of them. You'll like Dorothea."

"What did you say her name was—Dorothea? What do I do? Do I just walk in? Sha'n't I feel a fearful ass? How much do I give her?"

"A guinea. You'd better write and make an appointment."

"All right," said Percy. "But I know I shall look a frightful fool."

You would hardly believe the trouble it took to bring him to the scratch. In the end I took him round myself and left him there, and about a week later I ran into him between the acts at the Gaiety. The old boy was beaming.

"Reggie," he said, "you did me the best turn anyone's ever done me, sending me to Mrs. Darrell."

"Mrs. Darrell?"

"You know—Dorothea. Her real name's Darrell. She's a widow. Her husband was in a line regiment, and left her without a penny. It's a frightfully pathetic story. Haven't time to tell you now. My boy, she's a marvel. She had hardly looked at my hand when she said, 'You will prosper in any venture you undertake.' And next day, by Jove, I popped down to the Booles and separated young Roderick from fourteen pounds seven and six. She's a wonderful woman. Did you ever see just that shade of hair?"

"I didn't notice her hair."

He gaped at me in a sort of petrified astonishment.

"You—didn't—notice—her—hair?" he gasped.

Just then the bell rang, and I had to nip back to my stall.

I can't fix the dates exactly, but it must have been about three weeks after this that I got a telegram, "Call Eaton Square immediately.—FLORENCE CRAYE."

She needn't have signed her name. I should have known who it was from by the wording. Ever since I was a kid Percy's sister Florence has oppressed me to the most fearful extent. Not that I'm the only one. Her brothers live in terror of her, I know. Especially Lord Weeting. He's never been able to get away from her, and it's absolutely broken his spirit. He's a mild, hopeless sort of ass, who spends all his time at Weeting and has never been known to come to London. He's writing a history of the family or something, I believe.

You see, events have conspired, so to speak, to let Florence do pretty much as she likes with them. The family affairs have got themselves into a bit of a muddle. Originally there was Percy's father, Lord Worplesdon; Percy's elder brother Edwin, who's Lord Weeting; Florence, and Percy. Lady Worplesdon has been dead some years. Then came the smash. It happened through Lord Worplesdon. Most people, if you ask them, will tell you that he is bang off his rocker, and I'm not sure they're not right. At any rate, one morning he came down to breakfast, lifted the first cover on the sideboard, said, in a despairing sort of way, "Eggs! Eggs! Eggs! Curse all eggs!" and walked out of the room. Nobody thought much of it till about an hour afterwards, when they found that he had packed a portmanteau, left the house, and caught the train to London. Next day they got a letter from him, saying that he was off to the Continent, never to return, and that all communications were to be addressed to his solicitors.

And from that day none of them had seen him. He wrote occasionally, generally from Paris, and that was all.

Well, directly news of this got about down swooped a series of aunts to grab the helm. They didn't stay long. Florence had them out, one after the other, in no time. If any lingering doubt remained in their minds, don't you know, as to who was going to be boss at Weeting, it wasn't her fault. Since then she has run the show.

I went to Eaton Square. It was one of the aunts' houses. There was no sign of the aunt when I called—she had probably climbed a tree and pulled it up after her—but Florence was in the drawing-room.

She is a tall woman with what, I believe, is called "a presence." Her eyes are bright and black, and have a way of getting right inside you, don't you know, and running up and down your spine. She has a deep voice. She is about ten years older than Percy's brother Edwin, who is six years older than Percy.

"Good afternoon," she said. "Sit down."

I poured myself into a chair.

"Reginald," she said, "what is this I hear about Percy?"

I said I didn't know.

"He says that you introduced him."

"Eh?"

"To this woman—this Mrs. Darrell."

"Mrs. Darrell?"

My memory's pretty rocky, and the name conveyed nothing to me.

She pulled out a letter.

"Yes," she said; "Mrs. Dorothy Darrell."

"Great Scott! Dorothea!"

Her eyes resumed their spine-drill.

"Who is she?"

"Only a palmist."

"Only a palmist!" Her voice absolutely boomed. "Well, my brother Percy is engaged to be married to her."

"Many happy returns of the day," I said.

I don't know why I said it. It wasn't what I meant to

say. I'm not sure I meant to say anything.

She glared at me. By this time I was pure jelly. I simply flowed about the chair.

"You are facetious, Reginald," she said.

"No, no, no!" I shouted. "It slipped out. I wouldn't be facetious for worlds."

"I am glad. It is no laughing matter. Have you any suggestions?"

"Suggestions?"

"You don't imagine it can be allowed to go on? The engagement must be broken, of course. But how?"

"Why don't you tell him he mustn't?"

"I shall naturally express my strong disapproval, but it may not be effective. When out of the reach of my personal influence my wretched brother is self-willed to a degree."

I saw what she meant. Good old Percy wasn't going to have those eyes patrolling his spine if he knew it. He meant to keep away and conduct this business by letter. There was going to be no personal interview with sister, if he had to dodge about London like a snipe.

We sat for a long time without speaking. Then I became rather subtle. I had a brain-wave and saw my way to making things right for Percy and at the same time squaring myself with Florence. After all, I thought, the old boy couldn't keep away from the ancestral for the rest of his life. He would have to go to Weeting sooner or later. And my scheme made it pleasant and easy for him.

"I'll tell you what I should do if I were you," I said. "I'm not sure I didn't read some book or see some play somewhere or other where they tried it on, and it worked all right. Chap got engaged to a girl and the family didn't like it, but, instead of cutting up rough, they pretended they didn't object, and had the chap and the girl down to stay with them. And then, after the chap had seen the girl with the home-circle as a background, don't you know, he came to the conclusion that the shot wasn't on the board, and broke off the engagement."

It seemed to strike her.

"I hardly expected so sensible a suggestion from you, Reginald," she said. "It is a very good plan. It shows that you really have a definite substratum of intelligence; and it is all the more deplorable that you should idle your way through the world as you do, when you might be performing some really useful work."

That was Florence all over. Even when she patted you on the head she did it with her knuckles.

"I will invite them down next week," she went on. "You had better come, too."

"It's awfully kind of you, but the fact is—"

"Next Wednesday. Take the three forty-seven."

I met Percy next day. He was looking happy but puzzled, like a man who has found a sixpence in the street and is wondering if there's a string tied to it. I congratulated him on his engagement.

"Reggie," he said, "a pretty rum thing has happened. I feel as if I'd trodden on the last step when it wasn't there. I've just had a letter from my sister Florence asking me to bring Dorothy to Weeting on Wednesday. Florence doesn't seem to mind the idea of the engagement a bit;

and I'd expected that I'd have to put myself under police protection. I believe there's a catch some-where."

I tapped him on the breast-bone.

"There is, Percy, old lovely," I said, "and I'll tell you what it is. I saw her yesterday, and I can give you the straight tip. She thinks that if you see Mrs. Darrell mingling with the home-circle, you'll see flaws in her which you don't see when you don't see her mingling with the home-circle, don't you see. Do you see now?"

He laughed—heroically, don't you know.

"I'm afraid she'll be disappointed. Love like mine is not dependent on environment."

Which wasn't bad, I thought, if it was his own.

I said good-bye to him and toddled along, rather pleased with myself. It seemed to me that I had handled his affairs in a pretty masterly manner for a chap who's supposed to be one of the biggest chumps in London.

Well, of course, the thing was an absolute frost, as I ought to have guessed it would be. Whatever could have induced me to think that a fellow like poor old Percy stood a dog's chance against a determined female like his sister Florence I can't imagine. It was like expecting a rabbit to put up a show with a python. From the very start there was only one possible end to the thing. To a woman like Florence, who had trained herself as tough as whalebone by years of scrapping with her father and occasional by-battles with aunts, it was as easy as killing rats with a stick.

I was sorry for Mrs. Darrell. She was a really good sort, and, as a matter of fact, just the kind of wife who would have done old Percy a bit of good. And on her own ground I shouldn't wonder if she might not have made a fight for it. But at Weeting, with the family portraits glaring at her from every wall, and a general atmosphere of chilly disapproval which would have taken the heart out of anyone who hadn't been brought up to it from childhood, she hadn't an earthly. Especially as poor old Percy was just like so much putty in Florence's hands when he couldn't get away from her. You could see the sawdust trickling out of Love's Young Dream in a steady flow.

I took Mrs. Darrell for a walk one afternoon, to see if I couldn't cheer her up a bit; but it wasn't much good. She hardly spoke a word till we were on our way home. Then she said, with a sort of jerk: "I'm going back to London to-morrow, Mr. Pepper."

I suppose I ought to have pretended to be surprised, but I couldn't work it.

"I'm afraid you've had a rotten time," I said. "I'm awfully sorry."

She laughed.

"Thank you," she said. "It's nice of you to be sympathetic instead of tactful. You're rather a dear, Mr. Pepper."

I hadn't any remarks to make. I whacked at a nettle with my stick.

"I shall break off my engagement after dinner, so that Percy can have a good night's rest. I'm afraid he has been brooding on the future a good deal. It will be a great relief to him."

"Oh, no," I said.

"Oh, yes. I know exactly how he feels. He thought he could carry me off, but he finds he overestimated his powers. He has remembered that he is a Weeting. I imagine that the fact has been pointed out to him."

"If you ask my opinion," I said—I was feeling pretty sore about it—"that blighted blighter Florence is an absolute blighter."

"My dear Mr. Pepper, I wouldn't have dreamt of asking your opinion on such a delicate subject. But I'm glad to have it. Thank you very much. Do I strike you as a vindictive woman, Mr. Pepper?"

"I don't think you do," I said.

"By nature I don't think I am. But I'm feeling a little vindictive just at present."

She stopped suddenly.

"I don't know why I'm boring you like this, Mr. Pepper," she said. "For goodness' sake, let's be cheerful. Say something bright."

I was going to have a dash at it, but she collared the conversation and talked all the rest of the way. She seemed to have cheered up a whole lot.

She left next day. I gather she pushed Percy as per schedule, for the old boy looked distinctly brighter, and Florence wore an off-duty expression and was quite decently civil. Mrs. Darrell bore up all right. She avoided Percy, of course, and put in most of the time talking to Edwin. He evidently appreciated it, for I had never seen him look so nearly happy before.

I popped back to London directly afterwards, and I

hadn't been there much more than a week when a most remarkably rum thing happened. Turning in at the Empire for half an hour one evening, whom should I meet but brother Edwin, quite fairly festive, with a fat cigar in his mouth.

"Halloa, Reggie!" he said. "What-ho, my lad!"

"What are you doing here?" I said.

"I had to come up to London to look up a life of Hilary de Whyttange at the British Museum. I believe the old buffer was a sort of connection."

"This isn't the British Museum."

"I was beginning to suspect as much. The difference is subtle, but well marked."

It struck me that there was another difference that was subtle but well marked, and that was the difference between the Edwin I'd left messing about over his family history a week before and the jovial buck who was blowing smoke in my face now.

"As a matter of fact," he said, "the British Museum would be all the better for a little of this sort of thing. It's too conservative. That's what's the trouble with the British Museum. What's the matter with having a ballet and a few performing dogs in the reading-room? It would brighten the place up and attract custom. Reggie, you're looking fatigued. There's a place at the end of that corridor expressly designed for supplying first-aid to the fatigued. Let me lead you to it."

I'm not given to thinking much as a rule, but I couldn't help pondering a bit over this meeting with Edwin. It's hard to make you see the remarkableness of the whole thing, for, of course, if you look at it in one way, there's nothing so frightfully rackety in smoking a cigar and drinking a whisky and soda. But then you have never seen Edwin. There are degrees in everything, don't you know. For Edwin to behave as he did with me that night was simply nothing more nor less than a frightful outburst, and it disturbed me. Not that I cared what Edwin did, as a rule, but I couldn't help feeling a sort of what-d'you-call-it?—a presentiment—that somehow, in some way I didn't understand, I was mixed up in it, or was soon going to be. I think the whole fearful family had got on my nerves to such an extent that the mere sight of any of them made me jumpy.

And, by Jove, I was perfectly right, don't you know. In a day or two along came the usual telegram from Florence, telling me to come to Eaton Square.

I was getting about full up with Eaton Square, and I made up my mind I wouldn't go near the place. But of course I did. When it came to the point I simply hadn't the common manly courage to keep away.

Florence was there in the drawing-room as before.

"Reginald," she said, "I think I shall go raving mad."

This struck me as a jolly happy solution of everybody's troubles, but I felt it was too good to be true.

"Over a week ago," she went on, "my brother Edwin came up to London to consult a book in the British Museum. I anticipated that this would occupy perhaps an afternoon, and was expecting him back by an early train next day. He did not arrive. He sent an incoherent telegram. But even then I suspected nothing." She paused. "Yesterday morning," she said, "I had a letter from my aunt Augusta."

She paused again. She seemed to think I ought to be impressed.

"Very jolly," I said.

Her eyes tied a bow-knot in my spine.

"Jolly! Let me read you her letter. No, I will tell you its contents. Aunt Augusta had seen Edwin lunching at the Savoy with a creature."

"A what?"

"My aunt described her. Her hair was of a curious dull-bronze tint."

"Your aunt's?"

"The woman's. It was then that I began to suspect: How many women with dull-bronze hair does Edwin know?"

"Great Scott! Why ask me?"

I had got used to being treated as a sort of "Hey, Bill!" by Florence, but I was hanged if I was going to be expected to be an encyclopædia as well.

"One," she said. "That appalling Darrell woman."

She drew a deep breath.

"Yesterday evening," she said, "I saw them together in a taximeter cab. They were obviously on their way to some theatre."

She fixed me with her eye.

"Reginald," she said, "you must go and see her the first thing to-morrow."

"What!" I cried. "Me? Why? Why me?"

"Because you are responsible for the whole affair. You

introduced Percy to her. You suggested that she should come to Weeting. Go to her tomorrow and ascertain her intentions."

"But—"

"The very first thing."

"But wouldn't it be better to collar Edwin and pump him?"

"I have made every endeavour to see Edwin, but he deliberately avoids me. His answers to my telegrams are willfully evasive."

There was no doubt that Edwin had effected a thorough bolt. He was having quite the holiday. Two weeks in sunny London, what? And from what I'd seen of him, he seemed to be thriving on it. I didn't wonder Florence had got rather anxious. She'd have been more anxious if she had seen him when I did. He'd got a sort of "London is *so* bracing" look about him which meant a whole lot of trouble before he trotted back to the fold.

Well, I started off to interview Mrs. Darrell, and, believe me, I didn't half like the prospect. I think they ought to train the District Messengers to do this sort of thing.

I found her alone. The rush-hour of clients hadn't begun.

"How do you do, Mr. Pepper?" she said. "How nice of you to call."

Very friendly, and all that. It made the situation dashed difficult for a chap, if you see what I mean.

"I say, you know," I said. "What about it, don't you know?"

"I certainly don't," she said. "What ought I to know about what?"

"Well, about Edwin—Lord Weeting," I said. "How do we go?"

She smiled.

"Oh! So you're an ambassador, Mr. Pepper?"

"I feel more like a bally ass. But as a matter of fact I did come to see if I could find out how things were running. What's going to happen?"

"Are you consulting me professionally? If so, you must show me your hand. Or perhaps you would rather I showed you mine?"

It was rather subtle, but I got on to it after a bit.

"Yes," I said, "I wish you would."

"Very well. Do you remember a conversation we had, Mr. Pepper, my last afternoon at Weeting? We came to the conclusion that I was rather a vindictive woman."

"By Jove! You're ragging old Edwin so as to score off Florence?"

She flushed a little.

"How very direct you are, Mr. Pepper How do you know I'm not very fond of Lord Weeting? At any rate, I'm very sorry for him."

"He's such a chump."

"But he's improving every day. Have you seen him? You must notice the difference?"

"There is a difference."

"He only wanted taking out of himself. I think he found Lady Florence's influence a little oppressive sometimes."

"No. But, I say," I said, "are you going to marry him?"

"I'm only a palmist. I don't pretend to be a clairvoyante. A marriage may be indicated in Lord Weeting's hand, but I couldn't say without looking at it."

"But, look here, I shall have to tell Lady Florence something definite, or she won't give me a moment's peace."

"Tell her Lord Weeting is of age. Surely that's definite enough?"

And I couldn't get any more out of her. I went back to Florence and reported. She got pretty excited about it.

"Oh, if I were a man!" she said.

I didn't see how that would have helped. I said so.

"I'd go straight to Edwin and *drag* him away. He is staying at his club. If I were a man I could go in and find him—"

"Not if you weren't a member," I said.

"And tell him what I thought of his conduct. As I'm only a woman, I have to wait in the hall while a deceitful small boy pretends to go and look for him."

It had never struck me before what a jolly sound institution a club was. Only a few days back I'd been thinking that the subscription to mine was a bit steep. But now I saw that the place earned every penny of the money.

"Have you no influence with him, Reginald?"

I said I didn't think I had. She called me something. Invertebrate, or something. I didn't catch it.

"Then there's only one thing to do. You must find my father and tell him all. Perhaps you may rouse him to a sense of what is right. You may make him remember that he has duties as a parent."

I thought it far more likely that I should make him remember that he had a foot. I hadn't a very vivid recollection of Lord Worplesdon. I was quite a kid when he made his great speech on the egg question and legged it for the Continent; but what I did recollect didn't encourage me to go and chat with him about the duties of a parent. As I remembered him, he was a rather large man with elephantiasis of the temper. I distinctly recalled one occasion when I was spending my summer holidays at Weeting and he found me trying to shave old Percy, then a kid of fourteen, with his razor.

"I shouldn't be able to find him," I said.

"You can get his address from his solicitors."

"He may be at the North Pole."

"Then you must go to the North Pole."

"But, I say—"

"Reginald!"

"Oh, all right."

I knew just what would happen. Parbury, Parbury, Parbury, and Stevens, the solicitors, simply looked at me as if I had been caught stealing milk-cans. At least, Stevens did. And the three Parburys would have done it, too, only they had been dead a good time. Finally, after drinking me in for about a quarter of an hour, Stevens said that if I desired to address a communication to his lordship care of this office, it would be duly forwarded. Good morning. Good morning. Anything further? No, thanks. Good morning. *Good* morning.

I handed the glad news on to Florence and left her to do what she liked about it. She went down and interviewed Stevens. I suppose he'd had experience of her. At any rate, he didn't argue. He yielded up the address in level time. Lord Worplesdon was in Paris, but was to arrive in London that night, and would doubtless be at his club.

It was the same club where Edwin was hiding from Florence. I pointed this out to her.

"There's no need for me to butt in, after all," I said. "He'll meet Edwin there, and they can fight it out in the smoking-room. You've only to drop him a line explaining the facts."

"I shall certainly communicate with him in writing, but nevertheless you must see him. I cannot explain everything in a letter."

"But doesn't it strike you that he may think it pretty bad gall—impertinence, don't you know—for a comparative stranger like me to be tackling a delicate family affair like this?"

"You will explain that you are acting for me."

"It wouldn't be better if old Percy sallied along instead?"

"I *wish* you to go, Reginald."

Well, of course, it was all right, don't you know, but I was losing a stone a day over the business. I was getting so light that I felt that, when Lord Worplesdon kicked me, I should just soar up to the ceiling like an air-balloon.

The club was one of those large clubs that look like prisons. I used to go there to lunch with my uncle, the one who left me his money, and I always hated the place. It was one of those clubs that are all red leather and hushed whispers.

I'm bound to say, though, there wasn't much hushed whispering when I started my interview with Lord Worplesdon. His voice was one of my childhood's recollections.

He was most extraordinarily like Florence. He had just the same eyes. I felt boneless from the start.

"Good morning," I said.

"What?" he said. "Speak up. Don't mumble."

I hadn't known he was deaf. The last time we'd had any conversation—on the subject of razors—he had done all the talking. This seemed to me to put the lid on it.

"I only said 'Good morning,'" I shouted.

"Good what? Speak up. I believe you're sucking sweets. Oh, good morning? I remember you now. You're the boy who spoiled my razor."

I didn't half like this re-opening of old wounds. I hurried on.

"I came about Edwin, Lord Worplesdon," I said.

" Who?"

"Edwin. Your son."

"What about him?"

"Florence told me to see you."

"Who?"

"Florence. Your daughter."

"What about her?"

All this comedy duo, business, mind you, as if we were bellowing at each other across the street. All round the room you could see old gentlemen shooting out of their chairs like rockets and dashing off at a gallop to write to the committee about it. Thousands of waiters had appeared from nowhere, and were hanging about dusting table-legs. If ever a business wanted to be discussed privately, this seemed to me to be it. And it was just about as private as a conversation through megaphones in Piccadilly Circus.

"Didn't she write to you?"

"I got a letter from her. I tore it up. I didn't read it."

Jolly, what? I began to understand what a shipwrecked Johnny must feel when he finds there's something gone wrong with the life-belt.

I thought I might as well get to the point and get it over.

"Edwin's going to marry a palmist," I said.

"Who the devil's Harry?"

"Not Harry. Marry. He's going to marry a palmist."

About four hundred waiters noticed a speck of dust on an ashtray at the table next to ours, and swooped down on it.

"Edwin is going to marry a palmist?"

"Yes."

"She must be mad. Hasn't she seen Edwin?"

And just then who should stroll in but Edwin himself. I sighted him and gave him a hail.

He curveted up to us. It was amazing, the way the fellow had altered. He looked like a two-year-old. Flower in his buttonhole, and a six-inch grin, and all that. Lord Worplesdon seemed surprised, too. I didn't wonder. The

Edwin he remembered was a pretty different kind of a chap.

"Halloa, dad!" he said. "Fancy meeting you here! Have a cigarette?"

He shoved out his case. Lord Worplesdon helped himself in a sort of dazed way.

"You *are* Edwin?" he said, slowly.

I began to sidle out. They didn't notice me. They had moved to a settee, and Edwin seemed to be telling his father a funny story. At least, he was talking and grinning, and Lord Worplesdon was making a noise like distant thunder, which I supposed was his way of chuckling. I slid out and left them.

Some days later Percy called on me. The old boy was looking scared.

"Reggie," he said, "what do doctors call it when you think you see things when you don't? Hal-something. I've got it, whatever it is. It's sometimes caused by overwork. But it can't be that with me, because I've not been doing any work. You don't think my brain's going or any bally rot like that, do you?"

"What do you mean? What's been happening?"

"It's like being haunted. I read a story somewhere of a fellow who kept thinking he saw a battleship bearing down on him. I've got it, too. Four times in the last three days I could have sworn I saw my father and Edwin. I saw them as plainly as I see you. And, of course, Edwin's at Weeting and father's on the Continent somewhere. Do you think it's some sort of a warning? Do you think I'm going to die?"

"It's all right, old man," I said. "As a matter of fact, they are both in London just now."

"You don't mean that? Great Scott, what a relief! But, Reggie, old top, it couldn't have been them really. The last time was at Covent Garden, and the chap I mistook for Edwin was wearing a false nose and dancing all by himself in the middle of the floor."

I admitted it was pretty queer.

I was away for a few days after that in the country. When I got back I found a pile of telegrams waiting for me. They were all from Florence, and they all wanted me to go to Eaton Square. The last of the batch, which had arrived that morning, was so jolly peremptory that I felt as if something had bitten me when I read it.

For a moment I admit I hung back. Then I rallied. There are times in a man's life when he has got to show a bit of the old bulldog British pluck, don't you know, if he wants to preserve his self-respect. I did then. My bag was still unpacked. I told my man to put it on a cab. And in about two ticks I was bowling off to Charing Cross. I left for France by the night boat.

About three weeks later I fetched up at Nice. You can't walk far at Nice without bumping into a Casino. The one I hit my first evening was the Casino Municipale, in the Place Massena. It looked more or less of a Home from Home, so I strolled in. There was quite a crowd round the *boule*-tables, and I squashed in. And when I'd worked through into the front rank I happened to look down the table, and there was Edwin, with a green Tyrolese hat hanging over one ear, clutching out for a lot of five-franc pieces which the croupier was steering towards him at the end of a rake.

I was feeling lonely, for I knew no one in the place, so I edged round in his direction.

Half-way there I heard my name called, and there was Mrs. Darrell.

I saw the whole thing in a flash. Lord Worplesdon hadn't done a thing to prevent it, and the marriage had taken place. And here they were on their honeymoon. I wondered what Florence was thinking of it.

"Well, well, here we all are," I said. "I've just seen Edwin. He seems to be winning."

"Dear boy!" she said. "He does enjoy it so. I think he gets so much more out of life than he used to, don't you?"

"Rather! May I wish you happiness?"

"Thank you so much, Mr. Pepper. I sent you a piece of the cake, but I suppose you never got it."

"Lord Worplesdon didn't make any objections, then?"

"On the contrary. He was more in favour of the marriage than anyone."

"And I'll tell you why," I said. "I'm rather a chump, you know, but I observe things. I bet he was grateful to you for taking Edwin in hand and making him human."

"Why, you're wonderful, Mr. Pepper. That is exactly what he said himself. It was that that first made us friends."

"And—er—Florence?"

She sighed.

"I'm afraid Florence has taken the thing a little badly.

But I hope to win her over in time. I want all my children to love me."

"All your what?"

"I think of them as my children, you see, Mr. Pepper. I adopted them as my own when I married their father. Did you think I had married Edwin? What a funny mistake! I am very fond of Edwin, but not in that way. No; I married Lord Worplesdon. We left him at our villa tonight, as he had some letters to get off. You must come and see us, Mr. Pepper. I always feel that it was you who brought us together, you know. I wonder if you will be seeing Florence when you get back? Will you give her my very best love?"

—Strand, August 1912

4. Rallying Round Old George

I THINK one of the rummiest affairs I was ever mixed up with in the course of a lifetime devoted to butting into other people's business was that affair of George Lattaker at Monte Carlo. I wouldn't bore you, don't you know, for the world, but I think you ought to hear about it.

We had come to Monte Carlo on the yacht *Circe*, belonging to an old sportsman of the name of Marshall. Among those present were myself, my man Voules, a Mrs. Vanderley, her daughter Stella, Mrs. Vanderley's maid Pilbeam, and George. My name is Pepper, by the way—Reggie Pepper.

George was a dear old pal of mine. In fact, it was I who had worked him into the party. You see, George was due to meet his Uncle Augustus, who was scheduled, George having just reached his twenty-fifth birthday, to hand over to him a legacy left by one of George's aunts, for which he had been trustee. The aunt had died when George was quite a kid. It was a date that George had been looking forward to; for, though he had a sort of income—an income, after-all, is only an income, whereas a chunk of o'goblins is a pile. George's uncle was in Monte Carlo, and had written George that he would come to London and unbelt; but it struck me that a far better plan was for George to go to his uncle at Monte Carlo instead. Kill two birds with one stone, don't you know. Fix up his affairs and have a pleasant holiday simultaneously. So George had tagged along, and at the time when the trouble started we were anchored in Monaco Harbour, and Uncle Augustus was due next day.

Looking back, I may say that, so far as I was mixed up in it, the thing began at seven o'clock in the morning, when I was aroused from a dreamless sleep by the dickens of a scrap in progress outside my state-room door. The chief ingredients were a female voice that sobbed and said: "Oh, Harold!" and a male voice "raised in anger," as they say, which after considerable difficulty, I identified as Voules's. I hardly recognized it. In his official capacity Voules talks exactly like you'd expect a statue to talk, if it could. In private, however, he evidently relaxed to some extent, and to have that sort of thing going on in my midst at that hour was too much for me.

"Voules!" I yelled.

Spion Kop ceased with a jerk. There was silence, then sobs diminishing in the distance, and finally a tap at the door. Voules entered with that impassive, my-lord-the-carriage-waits look which is what I pay him for. You wouldn't have believed he had a drop of any sort of emotion in him.

"Voules," I said, "are you under the delusion that I'm going to be Queen of the May? You've called me early all right. It's only just seven."

"I understood you to summon me, sir."

"I summoned you to find out why you were making that infernal noise outside."

"I owe you an apology, sir. I am afraid that in the 'eat of the moment I raised my voice."

"It's a wonder you didn't raise the roof. Who was that with you?"

"Miss Pilbeam, sir; Mrs. Vanderley's maid."

"What was all the trouble about?"

"I was breaking our engagement, sir."

I couldn't help gaping. Somehow one didn't associate Voules with engagements. Then it struck me that I'd no right to butt in on his secret sorrows, so I switched the conversation.

"I think I'll get up," I said.

"Yes, sir."

"I can't wait to breakfast with the rest. Can you get me some right away?"

"Yes, sir."

So I had a solitary breakfast and went up on deck to smoke. It was a lovely morning. Blue sea, gleaming Casino, cloudless sky, and all the rest of the hippodrome. Presently the others began to trickle up. Stella Vanderley was one of the first. I thought she looked a bit pale and tired. She said she hadn't slept well. That accounted for it.

Unless you get your eight hours, where are you?

"Seen George?" I asked.

I couldn't help thinking the name seemed to freeze her a bit. Which was queer, because all the voyage she and George had been particularly close pals. In fact, at any moment I expected George to come to me and slip his little hand in mine, and whisper: "I've done it, old scout; she loves muh!"

"I have not seen Mr. Lattaker," she said.

I didn't pursue the subject. George's stock was apparently low that a.m.

The next item in the day's programme occurred a few minutes later when the morning papers arrived.

Mrs. Vanderley opened hers and gave a scream.

"The poor, dear Prince!" she said.

"What a shocking thing!" said old Marshall.

"I knew him in Vienna," said Mrs. Vanderley. "He waltzed divinely."

Then I got at mine and saw what they were talking about. The paper was full of it. It seemed that late the night before His Serene Highness the Prince of Saxburg-Liegnitz (I always wonder why they call these chaps "Serene") had been murderously assaulted in a dark street on his way back from the Casino to his yacht. Apparently he had developed the habit of going about without an escort, and some rough-neck, taking advantage of this, had laid for him and slugged him with considerable vim. The Prince had been found lying pretty well beaten up and insensible in the street by a passing pedestrian, and had been taken back to his yacht, where he still lay unconscious.

"This is going to do somebody no good," I said. "What do you get for slugging a Serene Highness? I wonder if they'll catch the fellow?"

" 'Later,' " read old Marshall, " 'the pedestrian who discovered His Serene Highness proves to have been Mr. Denman Sturgis, the eminent private investigator. Mr. Sturgis has offered his services to the police, and is understood to be in possession of a most important clue.' That's the fellow who had charge of that kidnapping case in Chicago. If anyone can catch the man, he can."

About five minutes later, just as the rest of them were going to move off to breakfast, a boat hailed us and came alongside. A tall, thin man came up the gangway. He looked round the group, and fixed on old Marshall as the probable owner of the yacht.

"Good morning," he said. "I believe you have a Mr. Lattaker on board—Mr. George Lattaker?"

"Yes," said Marshall. "He's down below. Want to see him? Whom shall I say?"

"He would not know my name. I should like to see him for a moment on somewhat urgent business."

"Take a seat. He'll be up in a moment. Reggie, my boy, go and hurry him up."

I went down to George's state-room.

"George, old man!" I shouted.

No answer. I opened the door and went in. The room was empty. What's more, the bunk hadn't been slept in. I don't know when I've been more surprised. I went on deck.

"He isn't there," I said.

"Not there!" said old Marshall. "Where is he, then? Perhaps he's gone for a stroll ashore. But he'll be back soon for breakfast. You'd better wait for him. Have you breakfasted? No? Then will you join us?"

The man said he would, and just then the gong went and they trooped down, leaving me alone on deck.

I sat smoking and thinking, and then smoking a bit more, when I thought I heard somebody call my name in a sort of hoarse whisper. I looked over my shoulder, and, by Jove, there at the top of the gangway, in evening dress, dusty to the eyebrows and without a hat, was dear old George.

"Great Scott!" I cried.

"'Sh!" he whispered. "Anyone about?"

"They're all down at breakfast."

He gave a sigh of relief, sank into my chair, and closed his eyes. I regarded him with pity. The poor old boy looked a wreck.

"I say!" I said, touching him on the shoulder.

He leaped out of the chair with a smothered yell.

"Did you do that? What did you do it for? What's the sense of it? How do you suppose you can ever make yourself popular if you go about touching people on the shoulder? My nerves are sticking a yard out of my body this morning, Reggie!"

"Yes, old boy?"

"I did a murder last night."

"What?"

"It's the sort of thing that might happen to anybody.

Directly Stella Vanderley broke off our engagement I—"

"Broke off your engagement? How long were you engaged?"

"About two minutes. It may have been less. I hadn't a stop-watch. I proposed to her at ten last night in the saloon. She accepted me. I was just going to kiss her when we heard someone coming. I went out. Coming along the corridor was that infernal what's-her-name—Mrs. Vanderley's maid—Pilbeam. Have you ever been accepted by the girl you love, Reggie?"

"Never. I've been refused dozens—"

"Then you won't understand how I felt. I was off my head with joy. I hardly knew what I was doing. I just felt I had to kiss the nearest thing handy. I couldn't wait. It might have been the ship's cat. It wasn't. It was Pilbeam."

"You kissed her?"

"I kissed her. And just at that moment the door of the saloon opened and out came Stella."

"Great Scott!"

"Exactly what I said. It flashed across me that to Stella, dear girl, not knowing the circumstances, the thing might seem a little odd. It did. She broke off the engagement, and I got out the dinghy and rowed off. I was mad. I didn't care what became of me. I simply wanted to forget. I went ashore. I—It's just on the cards that I may have drowned my sorrows a bit. Anyhow, I don't remember a thing, except that I can recollect having the deuce of a scrap with somebody in a dark street and somebody falling, and myself falling, and myself legging it for all I was worth. I woke up this morning in the Casino gardens. I've lost my hat."

I dived for the paper.

"Read," I said. "It's all there."

He read.

"Good heavens!" he said.

"You didn't do a thing to His Serene Nibs, did you?"

"Reggie, this is awful."

"Cheer up. They say he'll recover."

"That doesn't matter."

"It does to him."

He read the paper again.

"It says they've a clue."

"They always say that."

"But— My hat!"

"Eh?"

"My hat. I must have dropped it during the scrap. This man, Denman Sturgis, must have found it. It had my name in it!"

"George," I said, "you mustn't waste time. Oh!"

He jumped a foot in the air.

"Don't do it!" he said, irritably. "Don't bark like that. What's the matter?"

"The man!"

"What man?"

"A tall, thin man with an eye like a gimlet. He arrived just before you did. He's down in the saloon now, having breakfast. He said he wanted to see you on business, and wouldn't give his name. I didn't like the look of him from the first. It's this fellow Sturgis. It must be."

"No!"

"I feel it. I'm sure of it."

"Had he a hat?"

"Of course he had a hat."

"Fool! I mean mine. Was he carrying a hat?"

"By Jove, he *was* carrying a parcel. George, old scout, you must get a move on. You must light out if you want to spend the rest of your life out of prison. Slugging a Serene Highness is *lèse-majesté*. It's worse than hitting a policeman. You haven't got a moment to waste."

"But I haven't any money. Reggie, old man, lend me a tenner or something. I must get over the frontier into Italy at once. I'll wire my uncle to meet me in—"

"Look out," I cried; "there's someone coming!"

He dived out of sight just as Voules came up the companion-way, carrying a letter on a tray.

"What's the matter?" I said. "What do you want?"

"I beg your pardon, sir. I thought I heard Mr. Lattaker's voice. A letter has arrived for him."

"He isn't here."

"No, sir. Shall I remove the letter?"

"No; give it to me. I'll give it to him when he comes."

"Very good, sir."

"Oh, Voules! Are they all still at breakfast? The gentleman who came to see Mr. Lattaker? Still hard at it?"

"He is at present occupied with a kippered herring, sir."

"Ah! That's all, Voules."

"Thank you, sir."

He retired. I called to George, and he came out.

"Who was it?"

"Only Voules. He brought a letter for you. They're all at breakfast still. The sleuth's eating kippers."

"That'll hold him for a bit. Full of bones." He began to read his letter. He gave a kind of grunt of surprise at the first paragraph.

"Well, I'm hanged!" he said, as he finished.

"Reggie, this is a queer thing."

"What's that?"

He handed me the letter, and directly I started in on it I saw why he had grunted. This is how it ran:

"MY DEAR GEORGE, I shall be seeing you to-morrow, I hope; but I think it is better, before we meet, to prepare you for a curious situation that has arisen in connection with the legacy which your father inherited from your Aunt Emily, and which you are expecting me, as trustee, to hand over to you, now that you have reached your twenty-fifth birthday. You have doubtless heard your father speak of your twin-brother Alfred, who was lost or kidnapped—which, was never ascertained—when you were both babies. When no news was received of him for so many years, it was supposed that he was dead. Yesterday, however, I received a letter purporting that he had been living all this time in Buenos Ayres as the adopted son of a wealthy South American, and has only recently discovered his identity. He states that he is on his way to meet me, and will arrive any day now. Of course, like other claimants, he may prove to be an impostor, but meanwhile his intervention will, I fear, cause a certain delay before I can hand over your money to you. It will be necessary to go into a thorough examination of credentials, etc., and this will take some time. But I will go fully into the matter with you when we meet. —Your affectionate uncle, AUGUSTUS ARBUTT."

I read it through twice, and the second time I had one of those ideas I do sometimes get, though admittedly a chump of the premier class. I have seldom had such a thoroughly corking brain-wave.

"Why, old top," I said, "this lets you out."

"Lets me out of half the darned money, if that's what you mean. If this chap's not an impostor—and there's no earthly reason to suppose he is, though I've never heard my father say a word about him—we shall have to split the money. Aunt Emily's will left the money to my father, or, failing him, his 'offspring.' I thought that meant me, but apparently there are a crowd of us. I call it rotten work, springing unexpected offspring on a fellow at the eleventh hour like this."

"Why, you chump," I said, "it's going to save you. This lets you out of your spectacular dash across the frontier. All you've got to do is to stay here and be your brother Alfred. It came to me in a flash."

He looked at me in a kind of dazed way.

"You ought to be in some sort of a home, Reggie."

"Ass!" I cried. "Don't you understand? Have you ever heard of twin-brothers who weren't exactly alike? Who's to say you aren't Alfred if you swear you are? Your uncle will be there to back you up that you have a brother Alfred."

"And Alfred will be there to call me a liar."

"He won't. It's not as if you had to keep it up for the rest of your life. It's only for an hour or two, till we can get this detective off the yacht. We sail for England tomorrow morning."

At last the thing seemed to sink into him. His face brightened.

"Why, I really do believe it would work," he said.

"Of course it would work. If they want proof, show them your mole. I'll swear George hadn't one."

"And as Alfred I should get a chance of talking to Stella and making things all right for George. Reggie, old top, you're a genius."

"No, no."

"You *are*."

"Well, it's only sometimes. I can't keep it up."

And just then there was a gentle cough behind us. We spun round.

"What the devil are you doing here, Voules?" I said.

"I beg your pardon, sir. I have heard all."

I looked at George. George looked at me.

"Voules is all right," I said. "Decent Voules! Voules wouldn't give us away, would you, Voules?"

"Yes, sir."

"You would?"

"Yes, sir."

"But, Voules, old man," I said, "be sensible. What would you gain by it?"

"Financially, sir, nothing."

"Whereas, by keeping quiet"—I tapped him on the chest—"by holding your tongue, Voules, by saying nothing about it to anybody, Voules, old fellow, you might gain a considerable sum."

"Am I to understand, sir, that, because you are rich and I am poor, you think that you can buy my self-respect?"

"Oh, come!" I said.

"How much?" said Voules.

So we switched to terms. You wouldn't believe the way the man haggled. You'd have thought a decent, faithful servant would have been delighted to oblige one in a little matter like that for a fiver. But not Voules. By no means. It was a hundred down, and the promise of another hundred when we had got safely away, before he was satisfied. But we fixed it up at last, and poor old George got down to his state-room and changed his clothes.

He'd hardly gone when the breakfast-party came on deck.

"Did you meet him?" I asked.

"Meet whom?" said old Marshall.

"George's twin-brother Alfred."

"I didn't know George had a brother."

"Nor did he till yesterday. It's a long story. He was kidnapped in infancy, and everyone thought he was dead. George had a letter from his uncle about him yesterday. I shouldn't wonder if that's where George has gone, to see his uncle and find out about it. In the meantime, Alfred has arrived. He's down in George's state-room now, having a brush-up. It'll amaze you, the likeness between them. You'll think it *is* George at first. Look! Here he comes."

And up came George, brushed and clean, in an ordinary yachting suit.

They were rattled. There was no doubt about that. They stood looking at him, as if they thought there was a catch somewhere, but weren't quite certain where it was. I introduced him, and still they looked doubtful.

"Mr. Pepper tells me my brother is not on board," said George.

"It's an amazing likeness," said old Marshall.

"Is my brother like me?" asked George amiably.

"No one could tell you apart," I said.

"I suppose twins always are alike," said George. "But if it ever came to a question of identification, there would be one way of distinguishing us. Do you know George well, Mr. Pepper?"

"He's a dear old pal of mine."

"You've been swimming with him perhaps?"

"Every day last August."

"Well, then, you would have noticed it if he had had a mole like this on the back of his neck, wouldn't you?" He turned his back and stooped and showed the mole. His collar hid it at ordinary times. I had seen it often when we were bathing together.

"Has George a mole like that?" he asked.

"No," I said. "Oh, no."

"You would have noticed it if he had?"

"Yes," I said. "Oh, yes."

"I'm glad of that," said George. "It would be a nuisance not to be able to prove one's own identity."

That seemed to satisfy them all. They couldn't get away from it. It seemed to me that from now on the thing was a walk-over. And I think George felt the same, for, when old Marshall asked him if he had had breakfast, he said he had not, went below, and pitched in as if he hadn't a care in the world.

Everything went right till lunch-time. George sat in the shade on the foredeck talking to Stella most of the time. When the gong went and the rest had started to go below, he drew me back. He was beaming.

"It's all right," he said. "What did I tell you?"

"What did you tell me?"

"Why, about Stella. Didn't I say that Alfred would fix things for George? I told her she looked worried, and got her to tell me what the trouble was. And then—"

"You must have shown a flash of speed if you got her to confide in you after knowing you for about two hours."

"Perhaps I did," said George modestly, "I had no notion, till I became him, what a persuasive sort of chap my brother Alfred was. Anyway, she told me all about it, and I started in to show her that George was a pretty good sort of fellow on the whole, who oughtn't to be turned down for what was evidently merely temporary insanity. She saw my point."

"And it's all right?"

"Absolutely, if only we can produce George. How much longer does that infernal sleuth intend to stay here? He seems to have taken root."

"I fancy he thinks that you're bound to come back

sooner or later, and is waiting for you."

"He's an absolute nuisance," said George.

We were moving towards the companion way, to go below for lunch, when a boat hailed us. We went to the side and looked over.

"It's my uncle," said George.

A stout man came up the gangway.

"Halloa, George!" he said. "Get my letter?"

"I think you are mistaking me for my brother," said George. "My name is Alfred Lattaker."

"What's that?"

"I am George's brother Alfred. Are you my Uncle Augustus?"

The stout man stared at him.

"You're very like George," he said.

"So everyone tells me."

"And you're really Alfred?"

"I am."

"I'd like to talk business with you for a moment."

He cocked his eye at me. I sidled off and went below.

At the foot of the companion-steps I met Voules.

"I beg your pardon, sir," said Voules. "If it would be convenient I should be glad to have the afternoon off."

I'm bound to say I rather liked his manner. Absolutely normal. Not a trace of the fellow-conspirator about it. I gave him the afternoon off.

I had lunch—George didn't show up—and as I was going out I was waylaid by the girl Pilbeam. She had been crying.

"I beg your pardon, sir, but did Mr. Voules ask you for

the afternoon?"

I didn't see what business if was of hers, but she seemed all worked up about it, so I told her.

"Yes, I have given him the afternoon off."

She broke down—absolutely collapsed. Devilish unpleasant it was. I'm hopeless in a situation like this. After I'd said, "There, there!" which didn't seem to help much, I hadn't any remarks to make.

"He s-said he was going to the tables to gamble away all his savings and then shoot himself, because he had nothing left to live for."

I suddenly remembered the scrap in the small hours outside my state-room door. I hate mysteries. I meant to get to the bottom of this. I couldn't have a really first-class valet like Voules going about the place shooting himself up. Evidently the girl Pilbeam was at the bottom of the thing. I questioned her. She sobbed.

I questioned her more. I was firm. And eventually she yielded up the facts. Voules had seen George kiss her the night before; that was the trouble.

Things began to piece themselves together. I went up to interview George. There was going to be another job for persuasive Alfred. Voules's mind had got to be eased as Stella's had been. I couldn't afford to lose a fellow with his genius for preserving a trouser-crease.

I found George on the foredeck. What is it Shakespeare or somebody says about some fellow's face being sicklied o'er with the pale cast of care? George's was like that. He looked green.

"Finished with your uncle?" I said.

He grinned a ghostly grin.

"There isn't any uncle," he said. "There isn't any Alfred. And there isn't any money."

"Explain yourself, old top," I said.

"It won't take long. The old crook has spent every penny of the trust money. He's been at it for years, ever since I was a kid. When the time came to cough up, and I was due to see that he did it, he went to the tables in the hope of a run of luck, and lost the last remnant of the stuff. He had to find a way of holding me for a while and postponing the squaring of accounts while he got away, and he invented this twin-brother business. He knew I should find out sooner or later, but meanwhile he would be able to get off to South America, which he has done. He's on his way now."

"You let him go?"

"What could I do? I can't afford to make a fuss with that man Sturgis around. I can't prove there's no Alfred when my only chance of avoiding prison is to be Alfred."

"Well, you've made things right for yourself with Stella Vanderley, anyway," I said, to cheer him up.

"What's the good of that now? I've hardly any money and no prospects. How can I marry her?"

I pondered.

"It looks to me, old top," I said at last, "as if things were in a bit of a mess."

"You've guessed it," said poor old George.

I spent the afternoon musing on Life. If you come to think of it, what a queer thing Life is! So unlike anything else, don't you know, if you see what I mean. At any moment you may be strolling peacefully along, and all the time Life's waiting around the corner to fetch you one. You can't tell when you may be going to get it. It's all dashed puzzling. Here was poor old George, as well-meaning a fellow as ever stepped, getting swatted all over the ring by the hand of Fate. Why? That's what I asked myself. Just Life, don't you know. That's all there was about it.

It was close on six o'clock when our third visitor of the day arrived. We were sitting on the afterdeck in the cool of the evening—old Marshall, Denman Sturgis, Mrs. Vanderley, Stella, George, and I—when he came up. We had been talking of George, and old Marshall was suggesting the advisability of sending out search-parties. He was worried. So was Stella Vanderley. So, for that matter, were George and I, only not for the same reason.

We were just arguing the thing out when the visitor appeared. He was a well-built, stiff sort of fellow. He spoke with a German accent.

"Mr. Marshall?" he said. "I am Count Fritz von Cöslin, equerry to His Serene Highness"—he clicked his heels together and saluted—"the Prince of Saxburg-Liegnitz."

Mrs. Vanderley jumped up.

"Why, Count," she said, "what ages since we met in Vienna! You remember?"

"Could I ever forget? And the charming Miss Stella, she is well, I suppose not?"

"Stella, you remember Count Fritz?"

Stella shook hands with him.

"And how is the poor, dear Prince?" asked Mrs. Vanderley. "What a terrible thing to have happened!"

"I rejoice to say that my high-born master is better. He has regained consciousness and is sitting up and taking nourishment."

"That's good," said old Marshall.

"In a spoon only," sighed the Count. "Mr. Marshall, with your permission I should like a word with Mr. Sturgis."

"Mr. Who?"

The gimlet-eyed sportsman came forward.

"I am Denman Sturgis, at your service."

"The deuce you are! What are you doing here?"

"Mr. Sturgis," explained the Count, "graciously volunteered his services—"

"I know. But what's he doing here?"

"I am waiting for Mr. George Lattaker, Mr. Marshall."

"Eh?"

"You have not found him?" asked the Count anxiously.

"Not yet, Count; but I hope to do so shortly. I know what he looks like now. This gentleman is his twin-brother. They are doubles."

"You are sure this gentleman is not Mr. George Lattaker?"

George put his foot down firmly on the suggestion.

"Don't go mixing me up with my brother," he said. "I am Alfred. You can tell me by my mole."

He exhibited the mole. He was taking no risks.

The Count clicked his tongue regretfully.

"I am sorry," he said.

George didn't offer to console him,

"Don't worry," said Sturgis. "He won't escape me. I shall find him."

"Do, Mr. Sturgis, do. And quickly. Find swiftly that noble young man."

"What?" shouted George.

"That noble young man, George Lattaker, who, at the risk of his life, saved my high-born master from the assassin."

George sat down suddenly.

"I don't understand," he said feebly.

"We were wrong, Mr. Sturgis," went on the Count. "We leaped to the conclusion—was it not so?—that the owner of the hat you found was also the assailant of my high-born master. We were wrong. I have heard the story from His Serene Highness's own lips. He was passing down a dark street when a ruffian in a mask sprang out upon him. Doubtless he had been followed from the Casino, where he had been winning heavily. My high-born master was taken by surprise. He was felled. But before he lost consciousness he perceived a young man in evening dress, wearing the hat you found, running swiftly towards him. The hero engaged the assassin in combat, and my high-born master remembers no more. His Serene Highness asks repeatedly, 'Where is my brave preserver?' His gratitude is princely. He seeks for this young man to reward him. Ah, you should be proud of your brother, sir!"

"Thanks," said George limply.

"And you, Mr. Sturgis, you must redouble your efforts. You must search the land; you must scour the sea to find George Lattaker."

"He needn't take all that trouble," said a voice from the gangway.

It was Voules. His face was flushed, his hat was on the back of his head, and he was smoking a fat cigar.

"I'll tell you where to find George Lattaker!" he shouted.

He glared at George, who was staring at him.

"Yes, look at me," he yelled. "Look at me. You won't be the first this afternoon who's stared at the mysterious stranger who won for two hours without a break. I'll be even with you now, Mr. Blooming Lattaker. I'll learn you to break a poor man's heart. Mr. Marshall and gents, this morning I was on deck, and I over'eard 'im plotting to put up a game on you. They'd spotted that gent there as a detective, and they arranged that blooming Lattaker was to pass himself off as his own twin-brother. And if you wanted proof, blooming Pepper tells him to show them his mole and he'd swear George hadn't one. Those were his very words. That man there is George Lattaker, Hesquire, and let him deny it if he can."

George got up.

"I haven't the least desire to deny it, Voules."

"Mr. Voules, if *you* please."

"It's true," said George, turning to the Count. "The fact is, I had rather a foggy recollection of what happened last night. I only remembered knocking someone down, and, like you, I jumped to the conclusion that I must have assaulted His Serene Highness."

"Then you are really George Lattaker?" asked the Count.

"I am."

"'Ere, what does all this mean?" demanded Voules.

"Merely that I saved the life of His Serene Highness the Prince of Saxburg-Liegnitz, Mr. Voules."

"It's a swindle!" began Voules, when there was a sudden rush and the girl Pilbeam cannoned into the crowd, sending me into old Marshall's chair, and flung herself into the arms of Voules.

"Oh, Harold!" she cried. "I thought you were dead. I thought you'd shot yourself."

He sort of braced himself together to fling her off, and then he seemed to think better of it and fell into the clinch.

It was all dashed romantic, don't you know, but there *are* limits.

"Voules, you're sacked," I said.

"Who cares?" he said. "Think I was going to stop on now I'm a gentleman of property? Come along, Emma, my dear. Give a month's notice and get your 'at, and I'll take you to dinner at Ciro's."

"And you, Mr. Lattaker," said the Count, "may I conduct you to the presence of my high-born master? He wishes to show his gratitude to his preserver."

"You may," said George. "May I have my hat, Mr. Sturgis?"

There's just one bit more. After dinner that night I came up for a smoke, and, strolling on to the foredeck, almost bumped into George and Stella. They seemed to be having an argument.

"I'm not sure," she was saying, "that I believe that a man can be so happy that he wants to kiss the nearest thing in sight, as you put it."

"Don't you?" said George. "Well, as it happens, I'm feeling just that way now."

I coughed and he turned round.

"Halloa, Reggie!" he said.

"Halloa, George!" I said. "Lovely night."

"Beautiful," said Stella.

"The moon," I said.

"Ripping," said George.

"Lovely," said Stella.

"And look at the reflection of the stars on the—"

George caught my eye.

"Pop off," he said.

I popped.

—Strand, December 1912

5. Doing Clarence a Bit of Good

HAVE you ever thought about—and, when I say thought about, I mean really carefully considered the question of—the coolness, the cheek, or, if you prefer it, the gall with which Woman, as a sex, fairly bursts? *I* have, by Jove! But then I've had it thrust on my notice, by George, in a way I should imagine has happened to pretty few fellows. And the limit was reached by that business of the Yeardsley "Venus."

To make you understand the full what-d'you-call-it of the situation, I shall have to explain just how matters stood between Mrs. Yeardsley and myself.

When I first knew her she was Elizabeth Shoolbred. Old Worcestershire family; pots of money; pretty as a picture. Her brother Bill was at Oxford with me. My name's Reggie Pepper, by the way.

I loved Elizabeth Shoolbred. I loved her, don't you know. And there was a time, for about a week, when we were engaged to be married. But just as I was beginning to take a serious view of life and study furniture catalogues and feel pretty solemn when the restaurant orchestra played "The Wedding Glide," I'm hanged if she didn't break it off, and a month later she was married to a fellow of the name of Yeardsley—Clarence Yeardsley, an artist.

What with golf, and billiards, and a bit of racing, and fellows at the club rallying round and kind of taking me out of myself, as it were, I got over it, and came to look on the affair as a closed page in the book of my life, if you know what I mean. It didn't seem likely to me that we should meet again, as she and Clarence had settled down in the country somewhere and never came to London, and I'm bound to own that, by the time I got her letter, the wound had pretty well healed, and I was to a certain extent sitting up and taking nourishment. In fact, to be absolutely honest, I was jolly thankful the thing had ended as it had done.

This letter I'm telling you about arrived one morning out of a blue sky, as it were. It ran like this:

"MY DEAR OLD REGGIE, What ages it seems since I saw anything of you. How are you? We have settled down here in the most perfect old house, with a lovely garden, in the middle of delightful country. Couldn't you run down here for a few days? Clarence and I would be so glad to see you. Bill is here, and is most anxious to meet you again. He was speaking of you only this morning. *Do* come. Wire your train, and I will send the car to meet you. —Yours most sincerely,

ELIZABETH YEARDSLEY.

"P.S. We can give you new milk and fresh eggs. Think of that!

"P.P.S. Bill says our billiard-table is one of the best he has ever played on.

"P.P.S.S. We are only half a mile from a golf course. Bill says it is better than St. Andrews.

"P.P.S.S.S. You *must* come!"

Well, a fellow comes down to breakfast one morning, with a bit of a head on, and finds a letter like that from a girl who might quite easily have blighted his life! It rattled me rather, I must confess.

However, that bit about the golf settled me. I knew Bill knew what he was talking about, and, if he said the course was so topping, it must be something special. So I went.

Old Bill met me at the station with the car. I hadn't come across him for some months, and I was glad to see him again. And he apparently was glad to see me.

"Thank goodness you've come," he said, as we drove off. "I was just about at my last gasp."

"What's the trouble, old scout?" I asked.

"If I had the artistic what's-its-name," he went on, "if the mere mention of pictures didn't give me the pip, I daresay it wouldn't be so bad. As it is, it's rotten!"

"Pictures?"

"Pictures. Nothing else is mentioned in this household. Clarence is an artist. So is his father. And you know yourself what Elizabeth is like when one gives her her head?"

I remembered then—it hadn't come back to me before that most of my time with Elizabeth had been spent in picture-galleries. During the period when I had let her do just what she wanted to do with me, I had had to follow her like a dog through gallery after gallery, though pictures are poison to me, just as they are to old Bill. Somehow it had never struck me that she would still be going on in this way after marrying an artist. I should have thought that by this time the mere sight of a picture would have fed her up. Not so, however, according to old Bill.

"They talk pictures at every meal," he said. "I tell you, it makes a chap feel out of it. How long are you down for?"

"A few days."

"Take my tip, and let me send you a wire from London. I go there to-morrow. I promised to play against the Scottish. The idea was that I was to come back after the match. But you couldn't get me back with a lasso."

I tried to point out the silver lining.

"But, Bill, old scout, your sister says there's a most corking links near here."

He turned and stared at me, and nearly ran us into the bank.

"You don't mean honestly she said that?"

"She said you said it was better than St. Andrews."

"So I did. Was that all she said I said?"

"Well, wasn't it enough?"

"She didn't happen to mention that I added the words, 'I don't think'?"

"No, she forgot to tell me that."

"It's the worst course in Great Britain."

I felt rather stunned, don't you know. Whether it's a bad habit to have got into or not, I can't say, but I simply can't do without my daily allowance of golf when I'm not in London.

I took another whirl at the silver lining.

"We'll have to take it out in billiards," I said. "I'm glad the table's good."

"It depends what you call good. It's half-size, and there's a seven-inch cut just out of baulk where Clarence's cue slipped. Elizabeth has mended it with pink silk. Very smart and dressy it looks, but it doesn't improve the thing as a billiard-table."

"But she said you said—"

"Must have been pulling your leg."

We turned in at the drive gates of a good-sized house standing well back from the road. It looked black and sinister in the dusk, and I couldn't help feeling, you know, like one of those Johnnies you read about in stories who are lured to lonely houses for rummy purposes and hear a shriek just as they get there. Elizabeth knew me well enough to know that a specially good golf course was a safe draw to me. Not to mention the billiard-table. And she had deliberately played on her knowledge. What was the game? That was what I wanted to know. And then a sudden thought struck me which brought me out in a cold perspiration. She had some girl down here and was going to have a stab at marrying me off. I've often heard that young married women are all over that sort of thing.

Certainly she had said there was nobody at the house but Clarence and herself and Bill and Clarence's father, but a woman who could take the name of St. Andrews in vain as she had done wouldn't be likely to stick at a trifle.

"Bill, old scout," I said, "there aren't any frightful girls or any rot of that sort stopping here, are there?"

"Wish there were," he said. "No such luck."

As we pulled up at the front door, it opened, and a woman's figure appeared.

"Have you got him Bill?" she said, which in my present frame of mind struck me as a jolly creepy way of putting it. The sort of thing Lady Macbeth might have said to Macbeth, don't you know.

"Do you mean me?" I said.

She came down into the light. It was Elizabeth, looking just the same as in the old days.

"Is that you, Reggie? I'm so glad you were able to come. I was afraid you might have forgotten all about it. You know what you are. Come along in and have some tea."

Have you ever been turned down by a girl who afterwards married and then been introduced to her husband? If so, you'll understand how I felt when Clarence burst on me. You know the feeling. First of all, when you hear about the marriage, you say to yourself, "I wonder what he's like." Then you meet him, and think, "There must be some mistake. She can't have preferred *this* to me!" That's what I thought when I set eyes on Clarence.

He was a little thin, nervous-looking chappie of about

thirty-five. His hair was getting grey at the temples and straggly on top. He wore pince-nez, and he had a drooping moustache. I'm no Bombardier Wells myself, but in front of Clarence I felt quite a nut. And Elizabeth, mind you, is one of those tall, splendid girls who look like princesses. Honestly, I believe women do it out of pure cussedness.

"How do you do, Mr. Pepper? Hark! Can you hear a mewing cat?" said Clarence. All in one breath, don't you know.

"Eh?" I said.

"A mewing cat. I feel sure I hear a mewing cat. Listen!"

While we were listening the door opened, and a white-haired old gentleman came in. He was built on the same lines as Clarence, but was an earlier model. I took him, correctly, to be Mr. Yeardsley, senior. Elizabeth introduced us.

"Father," said Clarence, "did you meet a mewing cat outside? I feel positive I heard a cat mewing."

'No," said the father, shaking his head; "no mewing cat."

"I can't bear mewing cats," said Clarence. "A mewing cat gets on my nerves!"

"A mewing cat is so trying," said Elizabeth.

"*I* dislike mewing cats," said old Mr. Yeardsley.

That was all about mewing cats for the moment. They seemed to think they had covered the ground satisfactorily, and they went back to pictures.

We talked pictures steadily till it was time to dress for

dinner. At least, they did. I just sort of sat around. Presently the subject of picture-robberies came up. Somebody mentioned the "Monna Lisa," and then I happened to remember seeing something in the evening paper, as I was coming down in the train, about some fellow somewhere having had a valuable painting pinched by burglars the night before. It was the first time I had had a chance of breaking into the conversation with any effect, and I meant to make the most of it. The paper was in the pocket of my overcoat in the hall. I went and fetched it.

"Here it is," I said. "A Romney belonging to Sir Bellamy Palmer—"

They all shouted "What!" exactly at the same time, like a chorus. Elizabeth grabbed the paper.

"Let me look! Yes. 'Late last night burglars entered the residence of Sir Bellamy Palmer, Dryden Park, Midford, Hants—'"

"Why, that's near here," I said. "I passed through Midford—"

"Dryden Park is only two miles from this house," said Elizabeth. I noticed her eyes were sparkling.

"Only two miles!" she said. "It might have been us! It might have been the 'Venus'!"

Old Mr. Yeardsley bounded in his chair.

"The 'Venus'!" he cried.

"They all seemed wonderfully excited. My little contribution to the evening's chat had made quite a hit.

Why I didn't notice it before I don't know, but it was not till Elizabeth showed it to me after dinner that I had my first look at the Yeardsley "Venus." When she led me up to it, and switched on the light, it seemed impossible that I could have sat right through dinner without noticing it. But then, at meals, my attention is pretty well riveted on the food-stuffs. Anyway, it was not till Elizabeth showed it to me that I was aware of its existence.

She and I were alone in the drawing-room after dinner. Old Yeardsley was writing letters in the morning-room, while Bill and Clarence were rollicking on the half-size billiard-table with the pink silk tapestry effects. All, in fact, was joy, jollity, and song, so to speak, when Elizabeth, who had been sitting wrapped in thought for a bit, bent towards me and said, "Reggie."

And the moment she said it I knew something was going to happen. You know that pre-what-d'you-call-it you get sometimes? Well, I got it then.

"What o?" I said, nervously.

"Reggie," she said, "I want to ask a great favour of you."

"Yes?"

She stopped down and put a log on the fire, and went on, with her back to me:

"Do you remember, Reggie, once saying you would do anything in the world for me?"

There! That's what I meant when I said that about the cheek of Woman as a sex. What I mean is, after what had happened, you'd have thought she would have preferred to let the dead past bury its dead, and all that sort of thing, what?

Mind you, I *had* said I would do anything in the world for her. I admit that. But it was a distinctly pre-Clarence remark. He hadn't appeared on the scene then, and it stands to reason that a fellow who may have been a perfect knight-errant to a girl when he was engaged to her doesn't feel nearly so keen on spreading himself in that direction when she has given him the miss-in-baulk and gone and married a man who reason and instinct both tell him is a decided blighter.

I couldn't think of anything to say but "Oh, yes."

"There is something you can do for me now, which will make me everlastingly grateful."

"Yes?" I said.

"Do you know, Reggie," she said, suddenly, "that only a few months ago Clarence was very fond of cats?"

"Eh! Well, he still seems—er—*interested* in them, what?"

"Now they get on his nerves. Everything gets on his nerves."

"Some fellows swear by that stuff you see advertised all over the—"

"No, that wouldn't help him. He doesn't need to take anything. He wants to get rid of something."

"I don't quite follow. Get rid of something?"

" 'The 'Venus,' " said Elizabeth.

She looked up and caught my bulging eye.

"You saw the 'Venus,' " she said.

"Not that I remember."

"Well come into the dining room."

We went into the dining-room, and she switched on

the lights.

"There," she said.

On the wall close to the door—that may have been why I hadn't noticed it before; I had sat with my back to it—was a large oil-painting. It was what you'd call a Classical picture, I suppose. What I mean is—well, you know what I mean. All I can say is that it's funny I *hadn't* noticed it.

"Is that the 'Venus'?" I said.

She nodded.

"How would like to have a look at that every time you sat down to a meal?"

"Well, I don't know. I don't think it would affect me much. I'd worry through all right."

She jerked her head impatiently.

"But you're not an artist," she said. "Clarence is."

And then I began to see daylight. What exactly was the trouble I didn't understand, but it was evidently something to do with the good old Artistic Temperament, and I could believe anything about that. It explains everything. It's like the Unwritten Law, don't you know, which you plead in America if you've done anything they want to send you to chokey for and you don't want to go. What I mean, is if you're absolutely off your rocker, but don't find it convenient to be scooped into the luny-bin, you simply explain that, when you said you were a teapot, it was just your Artistic Temperament, and they apologize and go away. So I stood by to hear just how the A. T. had affected Clarence, the Cat's Friend, ready for anything.

And, believe me, it had hit Clarence badly.

It was this way. It seemed that old Yeardsley was an amateur artist and that this "Venus" was his masterpiece. He said so, and he ought to have known. Well, when Clarence married, he had given it to him as a wedding-present, and had hung it where it stood with his own hands. All right so far, what? But mark the sequel. Temperamental Clarence, being a professional artist and consequently some streets ahead of the dad at the game, saw flaws in the "Venus." He couldn't stand it at any price. He didn't like the drawing. He didn't like the expression of the face. He didn't like the colouring. In fact, it made him feel quite ill to look at it. Yet, being devoted to his father and wanting to do anything rather than give him pain, he had not been able to bring himself to store the thing in the cellar, and the strain of confronting the picture three times a day had begun to tell on him to such an extent that Elizabeth felt something had to be done.

"Now you see," she said.

"In a way," I said. "But don't you think it's making rather heavy weather over a trifle?"

"Oh, can't you understand? Look!" Her voice dropped as if she was in church, and she switched on another light. It shone on the picture next to old Yeardsley's. "There!" she said. "Clarence painted *that!*"

She looked at me expectantly, as if she were waiting for me to swoon, or yell, or something. I took a steady look at Clarence's effort. It was another Classical picture. It seemed to me very much like the other one.

Some sort of art criticism was evidently expected of me, so I made a dash at it.

"Er—'Venus'?" I said.

Mark you, Sherlock Holmes would have made the same mistake. On the evidence, I mean.

"No. 'Jocund Spring,'" she snapped. She switched off the light. "I see you don't understand even now. You never had any taste about pictures. When we used to go to the galleries together, you would far rather have been at your club."

This was so absolutely true that I had no remark to make. She came up to me, and put her hand on my arm.

"I'm sorry, Reggie. I didn't mean to be cross. Only I do want to make you understand that Clarence is *suffering*. Suppose—suppose—well, let us take the case of a great musician. Suppose a great musician had to sit and listen to a cheap, vulgar tune—the same tune—day after day, day after day, wouldn't you expect his nerves to break? Well, it is just like that with Clarence. Now do you see?"

"Yes, but—"

"But what? Surely I've put it plainly enough?"

"Yes. But what I mean is, where do I come in? What do you want me to do?"

"I want you to steal the 'Venus.'"

I looked at her.

"You want me to—?"

"Steal it. Reggie!" Her eyes were shining with excitement. "Don't you see? It's Providence. When I asked you to come here, I had just got the idea. I knew I could rely on you. And then by a miracle this robbery of the Romney takes place at a house not two miles away. It removes the last chance of the poor old man suspecting anything and having his feelings hurt. Why, it's the most wonderful compliment to him. Think! One night thieves steal a splendid Romney; the next the same gang take his 'Venus.' It will be the proudest moment of his life. Do it to-night, Reggie. I'll give you a sharp knife. You simply cut the canvas out of the frame, and it's done."

"But one moment," I said. "I'd be delighted to be of any use to you, but in a purely family affair like this, wouldn't it be better—in fact, how about tackling old Bill on the subject?"

"I have asked Bill already. Yesterday. He refused."

"But if I'm caught?"

"You can't be. All you have to do is to take the picture, open one of the windows, leave it open, and go back to your room."

It sounded simple enough.

"And as to the picture itself—when I've got it?"

"Burn it. I'll see that you have a good fire in your room."

"But—"

She looked at me. She always did have the most wonderful eyes.

"Reggie," she said; nothing more. Just "Reggie."

She looked at me.

Well, after all, if you see what I mean— The days that are no more, don't you know. Auld Lang Syne, and all that sort of thing. You follow me?

"All right," I said. "I'll do it."

I don't know if you happen to be one of those Johnnies who are steeped in crime, and so forth, and think nothing of pinching diamond necklaces. If you're not, you'll understand that I felt a lot less keen on the job I'd taken on when I sat in my room, waiting to get busy, than I had done when I promised to tackle it in the dining-room. On paper it all seemed easy enough, but I couldn't help feeling there was a catch somewhere, and I've never known time pass slower. The kick-off was scheduled for one o'clock in the morning, when the household might be expected to be pretty sound asleep, but at a quarter to I couldn't stand it any longer. I lit the lantern I had taken from Bill's bicycle, took a grip of my knife, and slunk downstairs.

The first thing I did on getting to the dining-room was to open the window. I had half a mind to smash it, so as to give an extra bit of local colour to the affair, but decided not to on account of the noise. I had put my lantern on the table, and was just reaching out for it, when something happened. What it was for the moment I couldn't have said. It might have been an explosion of some sort or an earthquake. Some solid object caught me a frightful whack on the chin. Sparks and things occurred inside my head, and the next thing I remember is feeling something wet and cold splash into my face, and hearing a voice that sounded like old Bill's say, "Feeling better now?"

I sat up. The lights were on, and I was on the floor, with old Bill kneeling beside me with a soda siphon.

"What happened?" I said.

"I am awfully sorry, old man," he said. "I hadn't a notion it was you. I came in here, and saw a lantern on the table and the window open and a chap with a knife in his hand, so I didn't stop to make inquiries. I just let go at his jaw for all I was worth. What on earth do you think you're doing? Were you walking in your sleep?"

"It was Elizabeth," I said. "Why, you know all about it. She said she had told you."

"You don't mean—"

"The picture. You refused to take it on, so she asked me."

"Reggie, old man," he said, "I'll never believe what they say about repentance again. It's a fool's trick and upsets everything. If I hadn't repented, and thought it was rather rough on Elizabeth not to do little thing like that for her, and come down here to do it after all, you wouldn't have stopped that sleep-producer with your chin. I'm sorry."

"Me, too," I said, giving my head another shake to make certain it was still on.

"Are you feeling better now?"

"Better than I was. But that's not saying much."

"Would you like some more soda-water? No? Well, how about getting this job finished and going to bed? And let's be quick about it too. You made a noise like a ton of bricks when you went down just now, and it's on the cards some of the servants may have heard. Toss you who carves."

"Heads."

"Tails it is," he said, uncovering the coin. "Up you get.

I'll hold the light. Don't spike yourself on that sword of yours."

It was as easy a job as Elizabeth had said. Just four quick cuts, and the thing came out of its frame like an oyster. I rolled it up. Old Bill had put the lantern on the floor and was at the sideboard, collecting whisky, soda, and glasses.

"We've got a long evening before us," he said. "You can't burn a picture of that size in one chunk. You'd set the chimney on fire. Let's do the thing comfortably. Clarence can't grudge us the stuff. We've done him a bit of good this trip. To-morrow'll be the maddest, merriest day of Clarence's glad New Year. On we go."

We went up to my room, and sat smoking and yarning away and sipping our drinks, and every now and then cutting a slice off the picture and shoving it in the fire till it was all gone. And what with the cosiness of it, and the cheerful blaze, and the comfortable feeling of doing good by stealth, I don't know when I've had a jollier time since the days when we used to brew in my study at school.

We had just put the last slice on when Bill sat up suddenly, and gripped my arm.

"I heard something," he said.

I listened, and, by Jove, I heard something, too. My room was just over the dining room, and the sound came up to us quite distinctly. Stealthy footsteps, by George! And then a chair falling over.

"There's somebody in the dining-room," I whispered.

There's a certain type of chap who takes a pleasure in positively chivvying trouble. Old Bill's like that. If I had been alone, it would have taken me about three seconds to persuade myself that I hadn't really heard anything after all. I'm a peaceful sort of cove, and believe in living and letting live, and so forth. To old Bill, however, a visit from burglars was pure jam. He was out of his chair in one jump.

"Come on," he said. "Bring the poker."

I brought the tongs as well. I felt like it. Old Bill collared the knife. We crept downstairs.

"We'll fling the door open and make a rush," said Bill.

"Supposing they shoot, old scout?"

"Burglars never shoot," said Bill.

Which was comforting provided the burglars knew it.

Old Bill took a grip of the handle, turned it quickly, and in he went. And then we pulled up sharp, staring.

The room was in darkness except for a feeble splash of light at the near end. Standing on a chair in front of Clarence's "Jocund Spring," holding a candle in one hand and reaching up with a knife in the other, was old Mr. Yeardsley, in bedroom slippers and a grey dressing-gown. He had made a final cut just as we rushed in. Turning at the sound, he stopped, and he and the chair and the candle and the picture came down in a heap together. The candle went out.

"What on earth?" said Bill.

I felt the same. I picked up the candle and lit it, and then a most fearful thing happened. The old man picked himself up, and suddenly collapsed into a chair and began to cry like a child. Of course, I could see it was only the Artistic Temperament, but still, believe me, it was devilish unpleasant. I looked at old Bill. Old Bill looked at me. We shut the door quick, and after that we didn't know what to do. I saw Bill look at the sideboard, and I knew what he was looking for. But we had taken the siphon upstairs, and his ideas of first aid stopped short at squirting soda-water. We just waited, and presently old Yeardsley switched off, sat up, and began talking with a rush.

"Clarence, my boy, I was tempted. It was that burglary at Dryden Park. It tempted me. It made it all so simple. I knew you would put it down to the same gang, Clarence, my boy. I—"

It seemed to dawn upon him at this point that Clarence was not among those present.

"Clarence?" he said, hesitatingly.

"He's in bed," I said.

"In bed! Then he doesn't know? Even now—Young men, I throw myself on your mercy. Don't be hard on me. Listen." He grabbed at Bill, who side-stepped. "I can explain everything—everything."

He gave a gulp.

"You are not artists, you two young men, but I will try to make you understand, make you realize what this picture means to me. I was two years painting it. It is my child. I watched it grow. I loved it. It was part of my life. Nothing would have induced me to sell it. And then Clarence married, and in a mad moment I gave my treasure to him. You cannot understand, you two young men, what agonies I suffered. The thing was done. It was irrevocable. I saw how Clarence valued the picture. I knew that I could never bring myself to ask him for it back. And yet I was lost without it. What could I do? Till this evening I could see no hope. Then came this story of the theft of the Romney from a house quite close to this, and I saw my way. Clarence would never suspect. He would put the robbery down to the same band of criminals who stole the Romney. Once the idea had come, I could not drive it out. I fought against it, but to no avail. At last I yielded, and crept down here to carry out my plan. You found me." He grabbed again, at me this time, and got me by the arm. He had a grip like a lobster. "Young man," he said, "You would not betray me? You would not tell Clarence?"

I was feeling most frightfully sorry for the poor old chap by this time, don't you know, but I thought it would be kindest to give it him straight instead of breaking it by degrees.

"I won't say a word to Clarence, Mr. Yeardsley," I said. "I quite understand your feelings. The Artistic Temperament, and all that sort of thing, I mean—what? *I* know. But I'm afraid— Well, look!"

I went to the door and switched on the electric light, and there, staring him in the face, were the two empty frames. He stood goggling at them in silence. Then he gave a sort of wheezy grunt.

"The gang! The burglars! They *have* been here, and they have taken Clarence's picture!" He paused. "It might have been mine! My Venus!" he whispered.

It was getting most fearfully painful, you know, but he had to know the truth.

"I'm awfully sorry, you know," I said. "But it *was*."

He started, poor old chap.

"Eh? What do you mean?"

"They *did* take your Venus."

"But I have it here."

I shook my head.

"That's Clarence's 'Jocund Spring,' " I said.

He jumped at it and straightened it out.

"What! What are you talking about? Do you think I don't know my own picture—my child—my 'Venus'? See! My own signature in the corner. Can you read, boy? Look: 'Matthew Yeardsley.' This is *my* picture!"

And—well, by Jove! It *was*, don't you know.

Well, we got him off to bed, him and his infernal 'Venus,' and we settled down to take a steady look at the position of affairs. Bill said it was my fault for getting hold of the wrong picture, and I said it was Bill's fault for fetching me such a crack on the jaw that I couldn't be expected to see what I was getting hold of, and then there was a pretty massive silence for a bit.

"Reggie," said Bill, at last, "how exactly do you feel about facing Clarence and Elizabeth at breakfast?"

"Old scout," I said, "I was thinking much the same myself."

"Reggie," said Bill, "I happen to know there's a milk-train leaving Midford at three-fifteen. It isn't what you'd call a flier. It gets to London at about half-past nine. Well—er—in the circumstances, how about it?"

—*Strand, May 1913*

6. Concealed Art

IF a fellow has lots of money and lots of time and lots of curiosity about other fellows' business, it is astonishing, don't you know, what a lot of strange affairs he can get mixed up in. Now, I have money and curiosity and all the time there is. My name's Pepper—Reggie Pepper. My uncle was the colliery-owner chappie, and he left me the dickens of a pile. And ever since the lawyer slipped the stuff into my hand and closed my fingers over it, whispering, "It's yours!" life seems to have been one thing after another.

For instance, the dashed rummy case of dear old Archie.

I first ran into old Archie when he was studying in Paris, and when he came back to London he looked me up, and we celebrated. He always liked me because I didn't mind listening to his theories of Art. For Archie, you must know, was an artist. Not an ordinary artist either, but one of those fellows you read about who are several years ahead of the times, and paint the sort of thing that people will be educated up to by about 1999 or thereabouts. What's the word? Futurists—that's it. Dear old Archie was a Futurist, and his trouble was that most of the fellows down Chelsea way, not being educated up to him, used to fling lay-figures and mahl-sticks and things at him when he uncorked his artistic theories, and this rather jarred on the poor old boy, so, whenever he wanted sympathy, he would come and talk to me, and I would sit and say, "Perfectly ripping, old lad!" at intervals, and he would go back to his studio feeling fit for work again. The consequence was that he got very much attached to me, and came to think a frightful lot of my good sense and judgment, which was how I got dragged into the thing I'm going to tell you about.

Mind you, I don't want to give you a wrong idea of old Archie. On every other subject except Art he was as sensible as you could wish. I have sat beside him at the Chelsea Football Ground, and absolutely marveled at the breadth and vigour of the way he talked of the referee when he didn't like the way he used the whistle, and he could imitate an Irish cook talking to an Italian organ-grinder better than anyone I have ever heard. It was only when he got on to the subject of his pictures that you felt like notifying the Commissioners in Lunacy.

Well, one day as I was sitting in the club, watching the traffic coming up one way and going down the other, and thinking of nothing in particular, in blew the old boy. He was looking rather worried.

"Reggie, I want your advice."

"You shall have it," I said. "State your point, old top."

"It's like this— I'm engaged to be married."

"My dear old scout, a million con—"

"Yes, I know. Thanks very much, and all that, but listen."

"What's the trouble? Don't you like her?"

A kind of rapt expression came over his face.

"Like her! Why, she's the only—"

He gibbered for a spell. When he had calmed down, I said, "Well then, what's your trouble?"

"Reggie," he said, "do you think a man is bound to tell his wife all about his past life?"

"Oh, well," I said, "of course, I suppose she's prepared to find that a man has—er—sowed his wild oats, don't you know, and all that sort of thing, and—"

He seemed quite irritated.

"Don't be a chump. It's nothing like that. Listen. When I came back to London and started to try and make a living by painting, I found that people simply wouldn't buy the sort of work I did at any price. Do you know, Reggie, I've been at it three years now, and I haven't sold a single picture."

I whooped in a sort of amazed way, but I should have been far more startled if he'd told me he had sold a picture. I've seen his pictures, and they are like nothing on earth. So far as I can make out what he says, they aren't supposed to be. There's one in particular, called "The Coming of Summer," which I sometimes dream about when I've been hitting it up a shade too vigorously.

It's all dots and splashes, with a great eye staring out of the middle of the mess. It looks as if summer, just as it was on the way, had stubbed its toe on a bomb. He tells me it's his masterpiece, and that he will never do anything like it again. I should like to have that in writing.

"Well, artists eat, just the same as other people," he went on, "and personally I like mine often and well cooked. Besides which, my sojourn in that dear Paris gave me a rather nice taste in light wines. The consequence was that I came to the conclusion, after I had been back a few months, that something had to be done. Reggie, do you by any remote chance read a paper called *Funny Slices?*"

"Every week."

He gazed at me with a kind of wistful admiration.

"I envy you, Reggie. Fancy being able to make a statement like that openly and without fear. Then I take it you know the Doughnut family?"

"I should say I did."

His voice sank almost to a whisper, and he looked over his shoulder nervously.

"Reggie, I do them."

"You what?"

"I do them—draw them—paint them. I am the creator of the Doughnut family."

I stared at him, absolutely astounded. I was simply dumb. It was the biggest surprise I had had in my life. Why, dash it, the Doughnut family was the best thing in its line in London. There is Pa Doughnut, Ma Doughnut, Aunt Bella, Cousin Joe, and Mabel, the daughter, and they have all sorts of slapstick adventures. Pa, Ma and Aunt Bella are pure gargoyles; Cousin Joe is a little more nearly semi-human, and Mabel is a perfect darling. I had often wondered who did them, for they were unsigned, and I had often thought what a deuced brainy fellow the chap must be. And all the time it was old Archie. I stammered as I tried to congratulate him.

He winced.

"Don't gargle, Reggie, there's a good fellow," he said. "My nerves are all on edge. Well, as I say, I do the Doughnuts. It was that or starvation. I got the idea one night when I had a toothache, and next day I took some specimens round to an editor. He rolled in his chair, and told me to start in and go on till further notice. Since then I have done them without a break. Well, there's the position. I must go on drawing these infernal things, or I shall be penniless. The question is, am I to tell her?"

"Tell her? Of course you must tell her."

"Ah, but you don't know her, Reggie. Have you ever heard of Eunice Nugent?"

"Not to my knowledge."

"As she doesn't sprint up and down the joy-way at the Hippodrome, I didn't suppose you would."

I thought this rather uncalled-for, seeing that, as a matter of fact, I scarcely know a dozen of the Hippodrome chorus, but I made allowances for his state of mind.

"She's a poetess," he went on, "and her work has appeared in lots of good magazines. My idea is that she would be utterly horrified if she knew, and could never be quite the same to me again. But I want you to meet her and judge for yourself. It's just possible that I am taking too morbid a view of the matter, and I want an unprejudiced outside opinion. Come and lunch with us at the Piccadilly tomorrow, will you?"

He was absolutely right. One glance at Miss Nugent told me that the poor old boy had got the correct idea. I hardly know how to describe the impression she made on me. On the way to the Pic. Archie had told me that what first attracted him to her was the fact that she was so utterly unlike Mabel Doughnut; but that had not prepared me for what she really was. She was kind of intense, if you know what I mean—kind of spiritual. She was perfectly pleasant, and drew me out about golf and all that sort of thing; but all the time I felt that she considered me an earthy worm whose loftier soul-essence had been carelessly left out of his composition at birth. She made me wish that I had never seen a musical comedy or danced on a supper table on New Year's Eve. And if that was the impression she made on me, you can understand why poor old Archie jibbed at the idea of bringing her *Funny Slices*, and pointing at the Doughnuts and saying, "Me—I did it!" The notion was absolutely out of the question. The shot wasn't on the board. I told Archie so directly we were alone.

"Old top," I said, "you must keep it dark."

"I'm afraid so. But I hate the thought of deceiving her."

"You must get used to that now you're going to be a married man," I said.

"The trouble is, how am I going to account for the fact that I can do myself pretty well—have most things, in fact, the same as mother used to make it?"

"Why, tell her you have private means, of course. What's your money invested in?"

"Practically all of it in B. and O. P. Rails. It is a devilish good thing. A pal of mine put me onto it."

"Tell her that you have a pile of money in B. and O. P., then. She'll take it for granted it's a legacy. A spiritual girl like Miss Nugent isn't likely to inquire further."

"Reggie, I believe you're right. It cuts both ways, that spiritual gag. I'll do it."

They were married quietly. I held the towel for Archie, and a spectacled girl with a mouth like a rat-trap, who was something to do with the Woman's Movement, saw fair play for Eunice. And then they went off to Scotland for their honeymoon. I wondered how the Doughnuts were going to get on in old Archie's absence, but it seemed that he had buckled down to it and turned out three months' supply in advance. He told me that long practice had enabled him to Doughnut almost without conscious effort. When he came back to London he would give an hour a week to them and do them on his head. Pretty soft! It seemed to me that the marriage was going to be a success.

One gets out of touch with people when they marry. I am not much on the social-call game, and for nearly six months I don't suppose I saw Archie more than twice or three times. When I did, he appeared sound in wind and limb, and reported that married life was all to the velvet, and that he regarded bachelors like myself as so many excrescences on the social system. He compared me, if I remember rightly, to a wart, and advocated drastic treatment.

It was perhaps seven months after he had told Eunice that he endowed her with all his worldly goods—she not suspecting what the parcel contained—that he came to me unexpectedly one afternoon with a face so long and sick-looking that my finger was on the button and I was ordering brandy and soda before he had time to speak.

"Reggie," he said, "an awful thing has happened. Have you seen the paper today?"

"Yes. Why?"

"Did you read the Stock Exchange news? Did you see that some lunatic has been jumping around with a club and hammering the stuffing out of B. and O. P.? This afternoon they are worth practically nothing."

"By jove! And all your money was in it. What rotten luck!" Then I spotted the silver lining. "But, after all, it doesn't matter so very much. What I mean is, bang go your little savings and all that sort of thing; but, after all, you're making quite a good income, so why worry?"

He gave me the sort of look a batsman gives the umpire when he gives him out leg-before-wicket.

"I might have known you would miss the point," he said. "Can't you understand the situation? This morning at breakfast Eunice got hold of the paper first. 'Archie,' she said, 'didn't you tell me all your money was in B. and O. P.?' 'Yes,' I said. 'Why?' 'Then we're ruined.' Now do you see? If I had had time to think, I could have said that

I had another chunk in something else, but I had committed myself. I have either got to tell her about those infernal Doughnuts, or else conceal the fact that I had money coming in."

"Great Scott! What on earth are you going to do?"

"I can't think. We can struggle along in a sort of way, for it appears that she has small private means of her own. The idea at present is that we shall live on them. We're selling the car, and trying to get out of the rest of our lease up at the flat, and then we're going to look about for a cheaper place, probably down Chelsea way, so as to be near my studio. What was that stuff I've been drinking? Ring for another of the same, there's a good fellow. In fact, I think you had better keep your finger permanently on the bell. I shall want all they've got."

The spectacle of a fellow human being up to his neck in the *consommé* is painful, of course, but there's certainly what the advertisements at the top of magazine stories call a "tense human interest" about it, and I'm bound to say that I saw as much as possible of poor old Archie from now on. His sad case fascinated me. It was rather thrilling to see him wrestling with New Zealand mutton-hash and draught beer down at his Chelsea flat, with all the suppressed anguish of a man who has let himself get accustomed to delicate food and vintage wines, and think that a word from him could send him whizzing back to the old life again whenever he wished. But at what a cost, as they say in the novels. That was the catch. He might hate this new order of things, but his lips were sealed.

He loathed it, poor old lad! He was an independent

sort of a chap, and the thought that he was living on his wife's money hit him pretty hard. And the food problem was almost as bad. I had him to lunch as often as he could come, and let him do the ordering, and afterwards, as we smoked and drank our coffee, he would tell me all the things that their cook could do—and did—with a leg of mutton. The way he described how she piloted it through to the fourth day in the shape of mince was one of the most moving things I have ever heard, by Jove it was!

I personally came in for a good deal of quiet esteem for the way in which I stuck to him in his adversity. I don't think Eunice had thought much of me before, but now she seemed to feel that I had formed a corner in golden hearts. I took advantage of this to try and pave the way for a confession on poor old Archie's part.

"I wonder, Archie, old top," I said one evening after we had dined on mutton-hash and were sitting round trying to forget it, "I wonder you don't try another line in painting. I've heard that some of these fellows who draw for the comic papers—"

Mrs. Archie nipped me in the bud.

"How can you suggest such a thing, Mr. Pepper? A man with Archie's genius! I know the public is not educated up to his work, but it is only a question of time. Archie suffers, like all pioneers, from being ahead of his generation. But, thank Heaven, he need not sully his genius by stooping—"

"No, no," I said. "Sorry. I only suggested it."

After that I gave more time than ever to trying to

think of a solution. Sometimes I would lie awake at night, and my manner towards Wilberforce, my man, became so distrait that it almost caused a rift. He asked me one morning which suit I would wear that day, and, by Jove, I said, "Oh, any of them. I don't mind." There was a most frightful silence, and I woke up to find him looking at me with such a dashed wounded expression in his eyes that I had to tip him a couple of quid to bring him round again.

Well, you can't go on straining your brain like that forever without something breaking loose, and one night, just after I had gone to bed, I got it. Yes, by gad, absolutely got it. And I was so excited that I hopped out from under the blankets there and then, and rang up old Archie on the phone.

"Archie, old scout," I said, "can the missis hear what I'm saying? Well then, don't say anything to give the show away. Keep on saying, 'Yes? Halloa?' so that you can tell her it was someone on the wrong wire. I've got it, my boy. All you've got to do to solve the whole problem is to tell her you've sold one of your pictures. Make the price as big as you like. Come and lunch with me tomorrow at the club, and we'll settle the details."

There was a pause, and then Archie's voice said, "Halloa, halloa?" It might have been a bit disappointing, only there was a tremble in it which made me understand how happy I had made the old boy. I went back to bed and slept like a king.

Next day we lunched together, and fixed the thing up. I have never seen anyone so supremely braced. We examined the scheme from every angle and there wasn't a flaw in it. The only difficulty was to hit on a plausible purchaser. Archie suggested me, but I couldn't see it. I said it would sound fishy. Eventually I had a brain wave, and suggested J. Bellingwood Brackett, the American millionaire. He lives in London, and you see his name in the papers everyday as having bought some painting or statue or something, so why shouldn't he buy Archie's "Coming of Summer"? And Archie said, "Exactly—why shouldn't he? And if he had had any sense in his fat head, he would have done it long ago, dash him!" Which shows you that dear old Archie was bracing up, for I've heard him use much the same language in happier days about a referee.

He went off, crammed to the eyebrows with good food and happiness, to tell Mrs. Archie that all was well, and that the old home was saved, and that Canterbury mutton might now be definitely considered as off the bill of fare.

He told me on the phone that night that he had made the price two thousand pounds, because he needed the money, and what was two thousand to a man who had been fleecing the widow and the orphan for forty odd years without a break? I thought the price was a bit high, but I agreed that J. Bellingwood could afford it. And happiness, you might say, reigned supreme.

Why is it that there is always a catch in these good things? Fellows who know—detectives and people like that—will tell you that nine times out of ten a murderer will go and make some fat-headed bloomer which leads to his being caught on the hop. He either does something, or forgets to take something into his calculations, with the result that, bing! he's copped. Putting up a game on anyone, even from the best motives, is rather like that. You think the whole thing over, and fancy that you've allowed for everything, and all the time you've forgotten to spot something that ought to have been absolutely obvious.

What Archie and I forgot to allow for was the fact that this thing might get into the papers.

But, mind you, even if we had remembered about the papers, I doubt if we should have revised the scheme much. We should have taken it for granted that, if they mentioned it at all, they would just have given it five lines somewhere in the "Items of Interest" column, between the news of the birth of a five-legged kitten in Wales and the announcement of the hundred and first birthday of someone in a Bermondsey workhouse.

Did they? They did not! They ran it on the middle page with illustrations and head-lines.

I don't know when I've had such a nasty jar as I got when Wilberforce brought me the paper in bed, and I languidly opened it and this jumped out and bit at me:

BELLINGWOOD BRACKETT DISCOVERS
ENGLISH GENIUS

———

PAYS STUPENDOUS PRICE
FOR YOUNG ARTIST'S PICTURE

———

HITHERTO UNKNOWN FUTURIST
RECEIVES £2,000

Underneath there was a column, some of it about Archie, the rest about the picture; and scattered over the page were two photographs of old Archie, looking more like Pa Doughnut than anything human, and a smudged reproduction of "The Coming of Summer"; and, believe me, frightful as the original of that weird exhibit looked, the reproduction had it licked to a whisper. It was one of the ghastliest things I have ever seen.

Well, after the first shock I recovered a bit. After all, it was fame for dear old Archie. As soon as I had had lunch I went down to the flat to congratulate him.

He was sitting there with Mrs. Archie. He was looking a bit dazed, but she was simmering with joy. She welcomed me as the faithful friend.

"Isn't it perfectly splendid, Mr. Pepper, to think that Archie's genius has at last been recognized? How quiet he kept it. I had no idea that Mr. Brackett was even interested in his work. I wonder how he heard of it?"

"Oh, these things get about," I said. "You can't keep a good man down."

"Think of two thousand pounds for one picture—and the first he has ever sold!"

"What beats me," I said, "is how the papers got hold of it."

"Oh, I sent it to the papers," said Mrs. Archie, in an offhand way.

"I wonder who did the writing up," I said.

"They would do that in the office, wouldn't they?" said Mrs. Archie.

"I suppose they would," I said. "They are wonders at

that sort of thing."

I couldn't help wishing that Archie would enter into the spirit of the thing a little more and perk up, instead of sitting there looking like a cod-fish. The thing seemed to have stunned the poor chappie. He told me afterwards that even then he had a sense of impending doom. He said he had a presentiment that there was more to come, and that Fate was just backing away and measuring the distance, preparatory to smiting him good and hard.

"After this, Archie," I said, "all you have to do is to sit in your studio, while the police see that the waiting line of millionaires doesn't straggle over the pavement. They'll fight—"

"What's that?" said Archie, starting as if someone had dug a red-hot needle into his calf.

It was only a ring at the bell, followed by a voice asking if Mr. Ferguson was at home.

"Probably an interviewer," said Mrs. Archie. "I suppose we shall get no peace for a long time to come."

The door opened, and the cook came in with a card. " 'Renshaw Liggett,' " said Mrs. Archie. "I don't know him. Do you, Archie? It must be an interviewer. Ask him to come in, Julia."

And in he came.

My knowledge of chappies in general, after a fairly wide experience, is that some chappies seem to kind of convey an atmosphere of unpleasantness the moment you come into contact with them. I don't know what it is about them—maybe it's something in the way they work their eyebrows—but directly you see them you feel that you want to get down into the bomb-proof cellar and lock the door after you.

Renshaw Liggett gave me this feeling directly he came in; and when he fixed me with a sinister glance and said, "Mr. Ferguson?" I felt inclined to say "Not guilty." I backed a step or two and jerked my head towards Archie, and Renshaw turned the searchlight off me and switched it onto him.

Renshaw Liggett was one of those sharp-cornered fellows—the sort of fellow you felt would give you a nasty gash if you ran against him in the street. His face worked outwards to a point at the end of his nose, like some kind of a bird. He had a sharp chin, and I didn't like the look of his eyes. Altogether, having given him the swift once-over, I was deuced glad that it was Archie he wanted a chat with and not me.

"You are Mr. Archibald Ferguson, the artist?"

Archie nodded pallidly, and Renshaw nodded, as much as to say that you couldn't deceive him. He produced a sheet of paper. It was the middle page of the *Mail*.

"You authorized the publication of this?"

Archie nodded again.

"I represent Mr. Brackett. The publication of this most impudent fiction has caused Mr. Brackett extreme annoyance, and, as it might also lead to other and more serious consequences, I must insist that a full denial be published without a moment's delay."

"What do you mean?" cried Mrs. Archie. "Are you mad?"

She had been standing, listening to the conversation in

a sort of trance. Now she jumped into the fight with a vim that turned Renshaw's attention to her in a second.

"No, madam, I am not mad. Nor, despite the interested assertions of certain parties whom I need not specify by name, is Mr. Brackett. It may be news to you, Mrs. Ferguson, that an action is even now pending in New York, whereby certain parties are attempting to show that my client, Mr. Brackett, is *non compos* and should be legally restrained from exercising control over his property. Their case, *qua* case, is extremely weak, for even if we admit their contention that our client did, on the eighteenth of June last, attempt to walk up Fifth Avenue in his pyjamas, we shall be able to show that his action was the result of an election bet. But as the parties to whom I have alluded will undoubtedly snatch at every straw in their efforts to prove that Mr. Brackett is mentally infirm, the prejudicial effect of this publication cannot be over-estimated. Unless Mr. Brackett can clear himself of the stigma of having given two thousand pounds for this extraordinary production of an absolutely unknown artist, the strength of his case must be seriously shaken. I may add that my client's lavish patronage of Art is already one of the main planks in the platform of the parties already referred to. They adduce his extremely generous expenditure in this direction as evidence that he is incapable of a proper handling of his money. I need scarcely point out with what sinister pleasure, therefore, they must have contemplated—this."

And he looked at "The Coming of Summer" as if it were a black beetle.

I must say, much as I disliked the blighter, I couldn't help feeling that he had right on his side. It hadn't occurred to me in quite that light before, but, considering it calmly now, I could see that a man who would disgorge two thousand of the best o'goblins for Archie's Futurist masterpiece might very well step straight into the nut factory, and no questions asked.

Mrs. Archie came right back at him, as game as you please.

"I am sorry for Mr. Brackett's domestic troubles, but my husband can prove without difficulty that he did buy the picture. Can't you, dear?"

Archie, extremely white about the gills, looked at the ceiling and at the floor and at me and Renshaw Liggett.

"No," he said finally. "I can't. Because he didn't."

"Exactly," said Renshaw, "and I must ask you to publish that statement in tomorrow's papers without fail." He rose, and made for the door. "My client has no objection to young artists advertising themselves, realizing that this is an age of strenuous competition, but he firmly refuses to permit them to do it at his expense. Good afternoon."

And he legged it, leaving behind him one of the most chunky silences I have ever been mixed up in. For the life of me, I couldn't see who was to make the next remark. I was jolly certain that it wasn't going to be me.

Eventually Mrs. Archie opened the proceedings.

"What does it mean?"

Archie turned to me with a sort of frozen calm.

"Reggie, would you mind stepping into the kitchen

and asking Julia for this week's *Funny Slices*? I know she has it."

He was right. She unearthed it from a cupboard. I trotted back with it to the sitting room. Archie took the paper from me, and held it out to his wife, Doughnuts uppermost.

"Look!" he said.

She looked.

"I do them. I have done them every week for three years. No, don't speak yet. Listen. This is where all my money came from, all the money I lost when B. and O. P. Rails went smash. And this is where the money came from to buy 'The Coming of Summer.' It wasn't Brackett who bought it; it was myself."

Mrs. Archie was devouring the Doughnuts with wide-open eyes. I caught a glimpse of them myself, and only just managed not to laugh, for it was the set of pictures where Pa Doughnut tries to fix the electric light, one of the very finest things dear old Archie had ever done.

"I don't understand," she said.

"I draw these things. I have sold my soul."

"Archie!"

He winced, but stuck to it bravely.

"Yes, I knew how you would feel about it, and that was why I didn't dare to tell you, and why we fixed up this story about old Brackett. I couldn't bear to live on you any longer, and to see you roughing it here, when we might be having all the money we wanted."

Suddenly, like a boiler exploding, she began to laugh.

"They're the funniest things I ever saw in my life," she

gurgled. "Mr. Pepper, do look! He's trying to cut the electric wire with the scissors, and everything blazes up. And you've been hiding this from me all that time!"

Archie goggled dumbly. She dived at a table, and picked up a magazine, pointing to one of the advertisement pages.

"Read!" she cried. "Read it aloud."

And in a shaking voice Archie read:

"You think you are perfectly well, don't you? You wake up in the morning and spring out of bed and say to yourself that you have never been better in your life. You're wrong! Unless you are avoiding coffee as you would avoid the man who always tells you the smart things his little boy said yesterday, and drinking SAFETY FIRST MOLASSINE for breakfast, you cannot be PERFECTLY WELL. It is a physical impossibility. Coffee contains an appreciable quantity of the deadly drug caffeine, and therefore—"

"I wrote *that*," she said. "And I wrote the advertisement of the Spiller Baby Food on page ninety-four, and the one about the Pre-eminent Breakfast Sausage on page eighty-six. Oh, Archie, dear, the torments I have been through, fearing that you would some day find me out and despise me. I couldn't help it. I had no private means, and I didn't make enough out of my poetry to keep me in hats. I learned to write advertisements four years ago at a correspondence school, and I've been doing them ever since. And now I don't mind your knowing, now that you have told me this perfectly splendid news. Archie!"

She rushed into his arms like someone charging in for a bowl of soup at a railway station buffet. And I drifted out. It seemed to me that this was a scene in which I was not on. I sidled to the door, and slid forth. They didn't notice me. My experience is that nobody ever does—much.

—Strand, February 1915

7. The Test Case

WELL-MEANING chappies at the club sometimes amble up to me and tap me on the wish-bone, and say "Reggie, old top,"—my name's Reggie Pepper—"you ought to get married, old man."

Well, what I mean to say is, it's all very well, and I see their point and all that sort of thing; but it takes two to make a marriage, and up to date I haven't met a girl who didn't seem to think the contract was too big to be taken on.

Looking back, it seems to me that I came nearer to rolling up the aisle with Ann Selby than with most of the others. In fact, but for circumstances over which I had no dashed control, I am inclined to think that we should have brought it off; and I'm bound to say that, now that what the poet chappie calls the first fine frenzy has been on the ice for awhile and I am able to consider the thing calmly, I am deuced glad we didn't. She was one of those strong-minded girls, and I hate to think of what she would have done to me.

At the time, though, I was frightfully in love, and, for quite a while after she definitely chucked me I lost my stroke at golf so completely that a child could have given me one a hole. I was all broken up, and I contend to this day that I was dashed badly treated.

Let me give you what they call the data.

One day I was lunching with Ann, and was just proposing to her as usual, when instead of simply refusing me, as she generally did, she fixed me with a thoughtful eye and kind of opened her heart.

"Do you know, Reggie, I am in doubt?"

"Give me the benefit of it," I said, which I maintain was pretty good on the spur of the moment, but didn't get a hand. She simply ignored it, and went on.

"I must be certain. Marriage is such a gamble. I have just been staying with my sister Hilda and her husband—"

"Dear old Harold Bodkin? I know him well. In fact, I've a standing invitation to go down there and stay as long as I like. Harold is one of my best pals. Harold is a topper. Good old Harold is—"

"I would rather you didn't eulogise him, Reggie. I am extremely angry with Harold. He is making Hilda perfectly miserable."

"What on earth do you mean? Harold wouldn't hurt a fly. He's one of those dreamy, sentimental asses who—"

"It is precisely his sentimentality which is at the bottom of the whole trouble. You know, of course, that Hilda is not his first wife?"

"That's right. His first wife died about five years ago."

"He still cherishes her memory."

"Very sporting of him."

"*Is* it! If you were a girl, how would you like to be married to a man who was always making you bear in mind that you were only number two in his affections; a man whose idea of a pleasant conversation was a string of anecdotes illustrating what a dear woman his first wife was; a man who expected you to upset all your plans if they clashed with some anniversary connected with his other marriage?"

"That does sound pretty rotten. Does dear old Harold do all that?"

"That's only a small part of what he does. Why, if you will believe me, every evening at seven o'clock he goes and shuts himself up in a little room at the top of the house, and meditates."

"What on earth does he do that for?"

"Apparently his first wife died at seven in the evening. There is a portrait of her in the room. I believe he lays flowers in front of it. And Hilda is expected to greet him on his return with a happy smile."

"Why doesn't she kick?"

"I have been trying to persuade her to, but she won't. Most women are door-mats, and Hilda's one of them. She just pretends she doesn't mind. She has a nervous, sensitive temperament, and the thing is slowly crushing her. Don't talk to me of Harold!"

Considering that she had started him as a topic, I thought this pretty unjust. I didn't want to talk of Harold.

I wanted to talk about myself.

"Well, what has all this got to do with your not wanting to marry me?" I said.

"Nothing, except that it is an illustration of the risks a woman runs when she marries a man of a certain type."

"Great Scott! You surely don't class me with Harold?"

"Yes, in a way you are very much alike. You have both always had large private means, and have never had the wholesome discipline of work; and consequently you have never had to exercise your brains. A man who has never done that is an unknown quantity; he may do anything absurd and irritating."

"But, dash it, Harold—on your showing—is an absolute lunatic. Why should you think that I would be anything like that?"

"There's always the risk."

A hot idea came to me.

"Look here, Ann," I said, "Suppose I do something which proves that I'm not the total chump you consider me, how about then? Suppose I pull off some wheeze which only a deuced brainy chappie could think of? Would you marry me then?"

"Certainly. What do you propose to do?"

"Do! What do I propose to do? Why, I propose—well, to be absolutely frank, at the moment I don't quite know."

"You never will know, Reggie. You're one of the idle rich, and your brain, if you ever had one, has atrophied. Better not worry yourself trying to think. Go on sitting in your club-window, watching the traffic and sucking a cane."

Well, that seemed to me to put the lid on it. I didn't mind a heart-to-heart talk, but this was mere abuse. I changed the subject.

"What would you like after that fish?" I said coldly.

You know how it is when you get an idea. For awhile it sort of simmers inside you, and then suddenly it sizzles up like a rocket, and there you are, right in amongst it. That's what happened now. I went away from that luncheon, vaguely determined to pull off some wheeze which would prove that I was Brainy Bill, but without any clear notion of what I was going to do. Side by side with this in my mind was the case of dear old Harold. When I wasn't brooding on the wheeze, I was brooding on Harold. I was fond of the good old lad, and I hated the idea of his slowly wrecking the home purely by being a chump. And all of a sudden the two things clicked together like a couple of chemicals, and there I was with a topping plan for killing two birds with one stone. Doing something like that would startle and impress Ann, and at the same time healing the breach between Harold and Hilda.

It was like this. I happened to be passing a big sweet-shop, and in an idle sort of way I recalled the old yarn they pitch to you when you're a kid, about how they make certain that the people who sell the stuff don't go pinching the stock. You know the idea? When a new hand is taken on in a sweet-shop, the boss tells him or her to go right ahead and help himself. "This is the life," says the new hand, and proceeds to cut a wide swathe through the stuff. By the end of the week he has had all the sweets he wants in a lifetime, and wouldn't touch so much as an acid drop if you offered him a handsome reward.

And I had hardly brooded over this yarn for more than a minute or so, when something seemed to say to me, "This is the stuff for dear old Harold."

You see what I mean? My idea was that, in a case like this, it's no good trying opposition. What you want is to work it so that the chappie chucks it of his own accord. You want to egg him on to overdoing the thing till he gets so that he says to himself: "Enough! Never again!" That was what was going to happen to Harold.

When you're going to do a thing, there's nothing like making a quick start. I wrote to Harold straight away, proposing myself for a visit; and Harold wrote back telling me to come right along.

Harold and Hilda lived alone in a large house in Hertfordshire. I believe they did a good deal of entertaining at times, but on this occasion I was the only guest. The only other person of note in the place was Ponsonby, the butler. It was a quiet little party, but it suited me all right.

Of course, if Harold had been an ordinary sort of chappie, what I had come to do would have been a pretty big order. I don't mind many things, but I do hesitate to dig into my host's intimate, private affairs. But Harold was such a simple-minded Johnnie, so grateful for a little sympathy and advice, that my job wasn't so very difficult.

It wasn't as if he minded talking about Amelia, which was his first wife's name. The difficulty was to get him to talk of anything else. I began to understand what Ann meant by saying it was rough on Hilda.

A child ought to have been able to see that it was beginning to jar on her; but dear old Harold was more like a child with water on the brain than anything else. He was pure chump, clean through. I have a pretty wide circle of friends—the majority of them more or less off their rockers—but good old Harold was unique in my experience.

As an instance of the sort of fellow he was: the first night I was down there I was roused out of a refreshing sleep at about four o'clock or some such frightful hour, and found Harold standing by my bedside.

"Sh!" he said. "Don't make a noise. Come on!"

I was out of bed with an Indian club in one hand and a poker in the other before he could speak again. As we legged it through the house in our bare feet I tried to keep in mind all I'd ever been told about burglars not shooting except as a last resort. We got on to the top floor, and up a ladder through a trap-door on to the roof, and I was just bracing myself for the conflict and hoping they were small burglars, when he grabbed me by the arm.

"Look!"

I jumped a foot and looked where he pointed. I could not see anything.

"Isn't it wonderful?"

"Isn't what wonderful?"

"The dawn, man! Look at it! All pink!"

And then we went back to bed again.

That was Harold.

I'm bound to say the old boy was clay in my hands. People call me a chump, but Harold was a super-chump, and I did what I liked with him. The second morning of my visit, after breakfast, he grabbed me by the arm.

"This way, Reggie. I'm just going to show old Reggie Amelia's portrait, dear."

There was a little room all by itself on the top floor. He explained to me that it had been his studio. At one time Harold used to do a bit of painting in an amateur way.

"There!" he said, pointing at the portrait. "I did that myself, Reggie. It's like dear Amelia, isn't it?"

I suppose it was, in a way. At any rate, you could recognize the likeness when you were told who it was supposed to be.

"Do you know, Reggie, old top, sometimes when I sit here I feel as if Amelia were back again."

"It would be a bit awkward for you if she was."

"How do you mean?"

"Well, old lad, you happen to be married to someone else."

A look of child-like enthusiasm came over his face.

"Reggie, I wouldn't talk about this to anyone else but you," he began.

It's my experience that the fellows who begin by saying that are always the chappies who, if they couldn't get anyone else to tell their most intimate private affairs to, would rush out and buttonhole a policeman. I'm convinced that poor old Harold talked Amelia to everyone he got within speaking distance of. It wasn't his fault—it was just the way he was built. "But you are such an old pal," he went on, "that it's different with you. Reggie, I want to tell you how splendid Hilda is. Lots of other women might object to my still cherishing Amelia's memory, but Hilda has been so nice about it from the beginning. She understands so thoroughly."

I hadn't much breath left after that, but I used what I had to say: "She doesn't object?"

"Not a bit," said Harold. "It makes everything so pleasant."

When I had recovered a bit, I said, "What do you mean by everything?"

"Well," he said, "for instance, I come up here every evening at seven, and—er—think for a few minutes."

"A few minutes!"

"What do you mean?"

"Well, a few minutes isn't long."

"But I always have my sherry and bitters at a quarter past."

"You could postpone it."

"And Ponsonby likes us to start dinner at seven-thirty."

"What on earth has Ponsonby to do with it?"

"Well, he likes to get off by nine, you know. I think he goes off and plays skittles at the inn. You see, Reggie, old man, living in the country as we do, we have to study Ponsonby a little. He's always on the verge of giving notice—in fact, it was only by coaxing him on one or two occasions that we got him to stay on—and he is such a treasure that I don't know what we should do if we lost him. But, if you think that I ought to stay longer—?"

"Certainly I do. You ought to do a thing like this properly, or not at all."

He sighed.

"It's a frightful risk, but in future we'll dine at eight."

So that was something accomplished. I knew Harold pretty well, and I had the feeling that, if this Amelia business could be made to inconvenience him it wouldn't be long before he came to the conclusion that it was a trifle rough on Hilda. There's nothing like a little discomfort for injecting sense into the sort of fellow old Harold was.

It seemed to me that there was a suspicion of a cloud on Ponsonby's shining morning face when the news was broken to him that for the future he couldn't unleash himself on the local skittling talent as early as usual, but he made no kick, and the new order of things began.

My next offensive movement I attribute to a flash of absolute genius.

I was glancing through a photograph album in the drawing-room before lunch, when I came upon a face which I vaguely remembered. It was one of those wide, flabby faces with bulging eyes, and something about it struck me as familiar. I consulted Harold, who came in at that moment.

"That?" said Harold. "That's Percy."

He gave a slight shudder.

"Amelia's brother, you know. An awful fellow. I haven't seen him for years."

Then I placed Percy. I had met him once or twice in the old days, and I had a brainwave. Percy! He was the card to play. I remembered him well now—a stupendous blighter! Percy was everything that poor old Harold disliked most. He was hearty at breakfast; a confirmed back-slapper; a fellow whose only topic of conversation was racing; a man who prodded you in the chest when he spoke to you. I recollected quite clearly that Harold had never been able to stand him at any price.

"You haven't seen him for years?" I said in a shocked voice.

"Thank heaven!" said Harold devoutly.

I put down the photograph album and looked at him in a deuced serious way.

"Then it's high time you asked him to come here."

Harold blenched.

"Reggie, old man, you don't know what you are saying. You can't remember Percy. I wish you wouldn't say these things, even in fun."

"I'm not saying it in fun. Of course, it's none of my business, but you have paid me the compliment of confiding in me about Amelia, and I feel justified in speaking. All I can say is that, if you cherish her memory as you say you do, you show it in a very strange way. How you can square your neglect of Percy with your alleged devotion to Amelia's memory, beats me. It seems to me that you have no choice. You must either drop the whole thing and admit that your love for her is dead, or else you must stop this infernal treatment of her favourite brother. You can't have it both ways."

He looked at me like a hunted stag.

"But, Reggie, old man! Percy! He asks riddles at breakfast."

"I don't care."

"Hilda can't stand him."

"What of it?"

"The last time I saw him he talked for nearly half-an-hour about the Liverpool Handicap."

"It doesn't matter. You must invite him. It's not a case of what you like or dislike. It's your duty."

He struggled with his feelings for a bit.

"Very well," he said in a crushed sort of voice.

At dinner that night he said to Hilda: "I'm going to ask Amelia's brother, Percy, down to spend a few days. It is so long since we have seen him."

Hilda didn't answer at once. She looked at him in rather a curious sort of way, I thought.

"Very well, dear," she said.

I was deuced sorry for the poor girl, but I felt like a surgeon. She would be glad later on, for I was convinced that in a very short while poor old Harold must crack under the strain, especially after I had sprung the *coup* which I was meditating for the very next evening.

It was, so to speak, the culminating *coup* of my campaign. I had been watching Harold pretty closely, and I could see that the alteration in his schedule had not been without its effects. A man who has been in the habit for years of taking a sherry and bitters at a quarter-past seven suffers terribly if you suddenly deprive him of it. I speak from experience. When I used to go and stay with my uncle—the one who left me all his money—I never got a look at one. He was a teetotaller, and if you wanted anything to put an edge on you before a meal, it had to be lime-juice. So I could take a line through my own sufferings and arrive at a fairly close estimate of what Harold was feeling.

I had him weak. With my next move I hoped to administer the knock out.

It was quite simple. Simple, that is to say, in its working; but a devilish brainy thing for a chappie to have thought out.

What it came to was, that if dear old Harold enjoyed meditating in front of Amelia's portrait, he was jolly well going to have all the meditating he wanted and a bit over; for my simple scheme was to lurk outside till he had gone into the little room on the top floor, and then, with the aid of one of those jolly little wedges which you use to keep windows from rattling, see to it that the old boy remained there till they sent out search parties.

There wasn't a flaw in my reasoning. When Harold didn't roll in at the sound of the dinner-gong, Hilda would take it for granted that he was doing an extra bit of meditating that night, and her pride would stop her sending out a hurry-call for him. As for Harold, when he found that all was not well with the door, he would probably yell with considerable vim. But it was odds against anyone hearing him. As for me, you might think that I was going to suffer owing to the probable postponement of dinner. Not so, but far otherwise; for on the night I had selected for the *coup* I was dining out at the neighbouring inn with my old pal, Freddie Meadows. It is true that Freddie wasn't going to be within fifty miles of the place on that particular night; but they weren't to know that.

Did I describe the peculiar isolation of that room on the top floor, where the portrait was? I don't think I did. It was, as a matter of fact, the only room in those parts, for in the days when he did his amateur painting old Harold was strong on the artistic seclusion business and hated noise, and his studio was the only room in use on that floor.

In short, to sum up, the thing was a "cert."

Punctually at ten minutes to seven I was in readiness on the scene. There was a recess with a curtain in front of it, a few yards from the door, and there I waited, fondling my little wedge, for Harold to walk up to allow the proceedings to start. It was almost pitch dark, and that made the time of waiting seem longer. Somehow it's always more of a job waiting in the dark. I didn't dare to strike a light and look at my watch, but I knew Harold was always on time, so there wasn't any necessity.

Presently—I seemed to have been there much longer than ten minutes—I heard steps approaching. They came past where I stood, and went on into the room. The door closed, and I hopped out and sprinted up to it, and the next moment I had the good old wedge under the wood—as neat a job as you could imagine. And then I strolled downstairs, and toddled off to the inn.

I didn't hurry over my dinner, partly because the browsing and sluicing at the inn was really astonishingly good for such a place, and partly because I wanted to give Harold plenty of time for meditation. I suppose it must have been a couple of hours or more when I finally turned in at the front door.

Somebody was playing the piano in the drawing-room. I hesitated for a moment whether to go in or not. It could only be Hilda who was playing, and I had doubts as to whether Hilda wanted company just then—mine, at any rate.

Eventually I decided to risk it, for I wanted to hear the latest about dear old Harold. So in I went; and it wasn't Hilda at all. It was Ann Selby.

"Hello," I said. "I didn't know you were coming down here."

It seemed so odd, don't you know, as it hadn't been more than ten days or so since her last visit.

"Good evening, Reggie," she said.

Have you ever noticed that when things have been happening, you can nearly always tell it in the way a person wishes you "Good evening" or "Good morning"? I remember once, when I was a kid, smashing a valuable Dresden china figure in my uncle's study overnight. Next day, when I came down to breakfast, he said, "Good morning, Reginald!" and, if you'll believe me, I was out of the house and up a tree before he had time even to touch the fringe of the Dresden china topic. I *knew*, don't you know! It was the same now. Only the emotion I spotted in the words wasn't wrath or resentment—or whatever it is that makes an old gentleman weighing two hundred pounds leg it like a mustang of the prairie after a kid of ten and try to get home on him with an oak walking-stick—it was triumph. And what Ann had to be triumphant about I couldn't see.

"What's been happening?" I asked.

"How do you know anything has been happening?"

"I guessed it."

She played a bar or two of "See the Conquering Hero Comes" with the soft pedal down, then swung round on the music-stool and smiled happily.

"Well, you're quite right, as it happens, Reggie. A good deal has been happening."

She went to the door, and looked out, listening. Then she shut it, and came back.

"Hilda has revolted!"

"Revolted?"

"Yes, put her foot down—made a stand—refused to go on meekly putting up with Harold's insane behaviour."

"I don't understand."

She gave me a look of pity.

"You always were so dense, Reggie. I will tell you the whole thing from the beginning. You remember what I spoke to you about, one day when we were lunching together? Well, I don't suppose you have noticed it—I know what you are—but things have been getting steadily worse. For one thing Harold insisted on lengthening his visits to the top room, and naturally Ponsonby complained. Hilda tells me that she had to plead with him to induce him to stay on.

"Well, Hilda, poor girl, is so long-suffering that she actually put up with that without a murmur. Then the climax came. I don't know if you recollect Amelia's brother, Percy? You must have met him when she was alive—a perfectly unspeakable person with a loud voice and overpowering manners. Suddenly, out of a blue sky, Harold announced his intention of inviting him to stay. It was the last straw. This afternoon I received a telegram from poor Hilda, saying that she was leaving Harold and coming to stay with me; and a few hours later the poor child arrived at my flat."

You mustn't suppose that I stood listening silently to this speech. Every time she seemed to be going to stop for breath, I tried to jump in and tell her that all these things which had been happening were not mere flukes, as she seemed to think, but parts of a deuced carefully planned scheme of my own. But you know how it is with girls—especially if, like Ann, they're used to speaking in public. They don't stop for breath; it doesn't seem to matter to them whether they have any air in their lungs or not; they can keep on talking by sheer will-power. Every time I tried to interrupt, Ann would wave me down, and carry on without so much as a semi-colon.

But at this point I did manage to get a word in.

"I know, I know, I know!" I said. "I did it all. It was I who suggested to old Harold that he should lengthen the meditations, and insisted on his inviting Percy to stay."

I had hardly got the words out, when I saw that they were not making the hit I had anticipated. She looked at me with an expression of absolute scorn, don't you know.

"Well, really, Reggie," she said at last. "I never had a very high opinion of your intelligence, as you know, hut this is a revelation to me. What motive you can have had, unless you did it in a spirit of pure mischief—" She stopped, and there was a glare of undiluted repulsion in her eyes. "Reggie! I can't believe it! Of all the things I loathe most a practical joker is the worst. Do you mean to tell me you did all this as a practical joke?"

"Great Scott, no! It was like this—"

I paused for a bare second to collect my thoughts, so as to put the thing clearly to her. I might have known what would happen. She dashed in and collared the conversation again.

"Well, never mind. As it happens there is no harm done. Quite the reverse in fact. Hilda left a note for Harold, telling him what she had done and where she had gone and why she had gone, and Harold found it. The result was that after Hilda had been with me for some time, in he came in a panic and absolutely grovelled before the dear child. It seems incredible, but apparently he had had no notion that his absurd behaviour had met with anything but approval from Hilda. He went on as if he was mad. He was beside himself. He clutched his hair and stamped about the room, and then he jumped at the telephone and rang his home up on the trunk, and got Ponsonby on the wire and told him to go straight to the little room on the top floor and take Amelia's portrait down. I thought that a little unnecessary, myself, but he was in such a whirl of remorse that it was useless to try and get him to be rational. So Hilda was consoled, and he calmed down, and we all came down here in the car. So you see—"

At this moment the door opened and in came Harold.

"I say—hello, Reggie, old man—I say, it's a funny thing, but we can't find Ponsonby anywhere."

There are moments in a chappie's life, don't you know, when Reason, so to speak, totters, as it were, on its bally throne. This was one of them. The situation seemed somehow to have got out of my grip. I suppose, strictly speaking, I ought, at this juncture, to have cleared my throat and said in an audible tone, "Harold, old top, *I* know where Ponsonby is." But somehow I couldn't. Something seemed to keep the words back. I just stood there and said nothing.

"Nobody seems to have seen anything of him," said Harold. "I wonder where he can have got to."

Hilda came in, looking so happy I hardly recognised her. I remember feeling how strange it was that anybody could be happy just then.

"*I* know," she said. "Of course! Doesn't he always go off to the inn and play skittles at this time?"

"Why, of course," said Harold. "So he does."

And he asked Ann to play something on the piano. And pretty soon we had settled down to a regular jolly musical evening.

I remember reading a story once of a chappie who murdered another chappie. and not being quite decided what to do with the body, tied it under the dining-room table, and left it there pending his final decision. I had often wondered how he felt, especially as it happened that he had to give a dinner-party in the room where the body was. Now I knew. He may have felt a trifle uncomfortable, but he hadn't anything on me.

Ann must have played a matter of two or three thousand tunes when Harold got up.

"By the way," he said, "I suppose Ponsonby did what I told him about the picture. Lets go and see."

"Oh, Harold, what does it matter?" said Hilda.

"Don't be silly, Harold," said Ann.

I would have said the same, only I couldn't say anything.

Harold wasn't to be stopped. He led the way out of the room and upstairs, and we all trailed after him.

We had just reached the top floor when Hilda stopped, and said "Hark!"

It was a voice.

"Hi!" it said. "Hi!"

Harold legged it to the door of the studio.

"Ponsonby!"

From within came the voice again, and I have never heard anything to touch the combined pathos, dignity, and indignation it managed to condense into two words.

"Yes, sir?"

"What on earth are you doing in there?"

"I came here, sir, in accordance with your instructions on the telephone, and—"

Harold rattled the door.

"The bally thing's stuck."

"Yes, sir."

"How on earth did that happen?"

"I could not say, sir."

"Kick the door, Ponsonby."

"Very good, sir."

A restrained kicking made itself heard.

"How *can* the door have stuck like this?" said Ann.

Somebody—I suppose it must have been me, though the voice didn't seem familiar—spoke: "Perhaps there's a wedge under it," said this chappie.

"A wedge? What do you mean?"

"One of those little wedges you use to keep windows from rattling, don't you know."

"But why—? You're absolutely right, Reggie, old man, there is."

Harold yanked it out, and flung the door open, and out came Ponsonby, looking like Lady Macbeth.

"I wish to give notice, sir," he said, "and I should esteem it a favour if I might go to the pantry and procure food; I am extremely hungry."

And he passed from our midst, with Hilda after him, saying, "But, Ponsonby! Be reasonable, Ponsonby!"

Ann Selby turned on me with a swish.

"Reggie," she said, "did *you* shut Ponsonby in there?"

"Well, yes, as a matter of fact, I did."

"But why?" cried Harold.

"Oh, I don't know."

"But, good heavens, man, you must have had a reason."

"Well, to be absolutely frank, old top," I said, "I thought it was you."

"You thought it was me? What did you want to lock me in for?"

I hesitated. It was a delicate business telling him the

idea. And, while I was hesitating, Ann jumped in.

"I can tell you why, Harold. It was because Reggie belongs to that sub-species of humanity known as practical jokers. This sort of thing is his idea of humour."

"Humour!" said Harold. "Losing us a priceless butler! If that's your idea of—"

Hilda came back, pale and anxious.

"Harold, dear, do come and help me reason with Ponsonby. He is in the pantry gnawing a cold chicken like a dog, and he only stops to say, 'I give notice.' Do come and entreat him to take a broad view of the thing."

"Yes," said Ann. "Go, both of you. I wish to speak to Reggie alone."

That's how I came to lose Ann. At intervals during her remarks I tried to put my side of the case, but it was no good. She wouldn't listen. And presently something seemed to tell me that now was the time to go to my room and pack. Half an hour later I slid silently into the night.

—Pearson's, December 1915

The Sporting Life of Joan Romney

1. The Wire-Pullers

IT'S a splendid thing to be seventeen and have one's hair up and feel that one cannot be kissed indiscriminately any more by sticky boys and horrid old gentlemen who "knew you when you were *that* high, my dear," or who nursed you on their knees when you were a baby. When I came down to dinner for the first time in a long frock and with my hair in a bun there was a terrific sensation. Father said, "My dear Joan!" and gasped. The butler looked volumes of respectful admiration. The tweeny, whom I met on the stairs, giggled like an idiot. Bob, my brother, who is a beast, rolled on the floor and pretended to faint. Altogether it was an event. Mr. Garnet, who writes novels and things and happened to be stopping with us for the cricket, asked me to tell him exactly how it felt to have one's hair up for the first time. He said it would be of the utmost value to him to know, as it would afford him a lurid insight into the feminine mind.

I said: "I feel as if I were listening to beautiful music played very softly on a summer night, and eating heaps of strawberries with plenty of cream."

He said, "Ah!"

But somehow I was not satisfied. The dream of my life was to spend the winter in town, as soon as I had put my hair up, and go to dances and theatres and things, and regularly come out *properly*, instead of lingering on in this out-of-the-way place (which is ducky in the spring and summer, but awful in the winter), with nobody to be looked at by except relations and father and the curate and village doctors, and that sort of people.

We knew lots of nice people in town who would have given me a splendid time; but father was always too lazy to go. He hates London really. What he likes is to be out of doors all day and every day all the year round with his gun or rod. And he loves cricket, too. So do I. That is to say, I like watching it. But you can't watch cricket in the winter.

It really wasn't fair of father to keep me stowed away in a place like Much Middlefold now that I was grown up. I spoke to him about it after dinner.

I said, "Father, dear, you *are* going to take me to town this winter, aren't you?"

He shied. It is the only word to express it. "Er—well, my dear—well, we'll see, we'll see."

Poor old father, he does hate London so. It always brings on his rheumatism or something, and he spends most of his time there, I believe, when he is really obliged to go up on business, mooning about Kensington Gardens, trying to make believe it's really the country. But there are times when one feels that other people's objections must give way. When a girl is pretty (I believe I am) and has nice frocks (I know I have), it is perfectly criminal not to let her go and show them in town. And I love dancing. I want to go to dances every night. And in Much Middlefold we have only the hunt ball, and perhaps, if we're lucky, two or three other dances. And you generally have to drive ten miles to them.

So I was firm.

I said, "Father, dear, why can't we settle it now, and then you could write and get a house in good time?"

He jibbed this time. He sat in his chair and said nothing.

"Will you, father?"

"But the expense—"

"You can let the Manor."

"And the land; I ought to be looking after it."

"Oh, but the tenant man who takes the house will do that. Won't you write to-night, father, dear? I'll write if you'll tell me what to say. Then you needn't bother to move."

Here an idea seemed to strike him. I noticed with regret that his face brightened.

"I'll tell you what, my dear," he said; "we will make a bargain."

"Yes," I said. I knew something horrid was coming.

"If I make fifty in the match on Monday, we will

celebrate the event by spending the winter in town, much as I shall dislike it. Those wet pavements always bring on my rheumatism; don't know why. Wet grass never does."

"And if you don't make fifty, father?"

"Why, then," he replied, cheerfully, "we'll stay at home and enjoy ourselves."

The match that was to be played on Monday was against Sir Edward Cave's team. Sir Edward was a nasty little man who had made a great deal of money somehow or other and been knighted for it. He always got together a house-party to play cricket, and it was our great match. Sir Edward was not popular in the county, but he took a great deal of trouble with the cricket, and everybody was glad to play in his park or watch their friends playing.

Father always played for Much Middlefold in this match. He had been very good in his time, and I heard once that, if only the captain had not had so many personal friends for whom he wanted places in the team, father would have played for Oxford against Cambridge in his last year. But, of course, he was getting a little old now for cricket, and the Castle Cave match was the only one in which he played.

He had made twenty-five last year against Sir Edward Cave's team, and everybody had said how well he played, so I thought he might easily do better this year and make double that score.

"And if you make fifty you really will take me to town? You'll promise faithfully?"

"*Foi de gentilhomme!* The word of a Romney, my dear Joan; and, mind, if I do not make fifty the subject must be dropped for the present year of grace. Next year the discussion may be re-opened; but for this winter there must be no further attempt at coaxing. You know that I am as clay in your hands, young woman, and you must not take an unfair advantage of my weakness."

I promised.

"And you really will try, father, to make fifty?"

"I can promise you that, my dear. It would take more than the thought of the horrors of London to make me get out on purpose."

So the thing was settled.

I went to see Bob about it before going to bed. Bob is a Freshman at Magdalen, so, naturally, he is much more conceited than any three men have any right to be. I suppress him when I can, but lately, in the excitement of putting my hair up, I had forgotten to give him much attention, and he had had a bad relapse.

I found him in the billiard-room with Mr. Garnet. He was sprawling over the table, trying to reach his ball without the rest, and looking ridiculous. I waited till he had made his stroke and missed the red ball, which he ought to have pocketed easily.

Then I said, "Bob!"

He said, "Well, what?"

I think he must have been losing, for he was in a very bad temper.

"I want to speak to you."

"Go ahead, then."

I looked at Mr. Garnet. He understood at once.

"I'm just going to run upstairs for a second, Romney,"

he said. "I want my pipe. Cigarettes are bad for the soul. I sha'n't be long."

He disappeared. "Well?" said Bob.

"Father says that if he makes fifty on Monday against the Cave he'll take me to London for the winter."

Bob lit another cigarette and threw the match out of the window.

"You needn't hurry to pack," he said.

"Don't you think father will make fifty?"

"He hasn't an earthly."

"He made twenty-five last year."

"Yes; but this year the Cave men have got a new pro. I don't suppose you have ever heard of him, but his name's Simpson—Billy Simpson. He played for Sussex all last season, and was eleventh in the first-class bowling averages. The governor may have been the dickens of a bat in his day, but I'll bet he doesn't stand up to Billy for many overs. As for getting fifty—"

Words failed him. I felt like a cat. I could have scratched somebody—anybody; I did not care whom. No wonder father had made the bargain so cheerfully. He knew he could only lose by a miracle.

"Oh, Bob!" I said. My despair must have been tremendous, for it touched even Bob. He said, "Buck up!"

I said, "I won't buck up. I think everybody's horrid."

"Look here," said Bob, anxiously—I could see by his face that he thought I was going to cry—"look here, chuck playing the giddy goat and going into hysterics and that sort of thing, and I'll give you a straight tip."

"Well?"

"This man Simpson—I have it on the highest authority—is in love with your maid—what's her name?"

"Saunders?"

"Saunders. At present it's a close thing between him and a chap in the village. So far it's anybody's race. Billy leads at present, because it's summer and he's a celebrity in the cricket season. But he must pull it off before the winter or he'll be pipped, because the other Johnny plays footer and is a little tin god in these parts directly footer begins. Why don't you get Saunders to square Billy and make him bowl the governor some tosh which he can whack about?"

"Bob," I cried, "you're an angel, and I'm going to kiss you!"

"Here, I say!" protested Bob. "Break away!"

While I was kissing him Mr. Garnet came back.

"They never do that to me," I heard him murmur, plaintively.

I spoke to Saunders while she was brushing my hair.

I said, "Saunders!"

"Yes, miss."

"Er—oh, nothing."

"Yes, miss."

There was a pause.

"Saunders!" I said.

"Yes, miss."

"Do you know Simpson, the cricket professional at Castle Cave?"

"Yes, miss."

Her face, reflected in the glass in front of me, grew pinker. It is always rather pink.

"He is very fond of you, isn't he?"

"He says so, miss."

She simpered—visibly.

"He would do anything for you, wouldn't he?"

"He says so, miss." Then, in a burst of confidence, "He said so in poetry once, miss."

We paused again.

"Saunders!" I said.

"Yes, miss."

"Would you like that almost new hat of mine? The blue chiffon one with the pink roses ?"

She beamed. I believe her mouth watered.

"Oh, yes, miss."

Then I set out my dark scheme. I explained to her, having first shown her how necessary it was to keep it all quite secret, that a visit to town that winter depended principally on whether Mr. Simpson bowled well or badly in the match on Monday. She held Simpson in the hollow of her hand. Therefore she must prevail upon him to bowl father a sufficient quantity of easy balls to allow him to make fifty runs. In return for these services he would win Saunders's favour, and Saunders would win the hat she coveted and also a trip to London.

Saunders quite saw it.

She said, "Yes, miss."

"You *must* make him bowl badly," I said.

"I'll do what I can, miss. And I do really think that Mr. Simpson will act as I tells him to."

Once more she simpered.

Father came back in very good spirits from practising at the village nets next day.

"I was almost in my old form, my dear," he said. "I was watching them all the way. Why, I am beginning to think I shall make that fifty after all."

I said, "So am I, father, dear."

Saunders had stirring news on the following night. It seemed that Mr. Simpson was in an awkward position.

"Sir Edward, miss," said Saunders, "who always behaves very handsome, Mr. Simpson says, has offered to give him a ten-pound note if he bowls so well that nobody of the Middlefold side makes fifty against Castle Cave."

Here was a blow. I could not imagine any love being proof against such a bribe. London seemed to get farther away as I listened.

"And what does Simpson——"

"Well, Mr. Simpson and me, miss, we talked it over, and I said, 'Oh, if you prefer Sir Edward's old money to a loving heart,' I said, 'why, then,' I said, 'all is over between us,' I said, 'and there's others I could mention who worships the ground I tread on, and wouldn't refuse me nothing,' I said. And Mr. Simpson, he said ten pounds was a lot of money and wasn't to be found growing on every bush. So I just tossed my head and left him, miss; but I shall be seeing him to-morrow, and then we shall find out if he still thinks the same."

The next bulletin of Mr. Simpson's state of mind was favourable. After a day of suspense Saunders was able to inform me that all was well.

"I walked out with Mr. Harry Biggs, miss, and Mr. Simpson he met us and he looked so black, and when I saw him again he said he'd do it, he said. Ho, he is jealous of me, miss."

Mr. Harry Biggs, I supposed, was the footballer rival.

I slept well that night and dreamed that I was dancing with Saunders at a house in Belgrave Square, while Mr. Simpson, who looked exactly like Bob, stood in a corner and stared at us.

It was a beautiful day on the Monday. I wore my pink sprigged muslin with a pink sash and the pink chiffon hat Aunt Edith sent from Paris. Fortunately, the sun was quite hot, so I was able to have my pink parasol up the whole time, and words can't express its tremendous duckiness.

The Cave team were practising when we arrived, and lots of people had come. The Cave man, who was wearing a new Panama, met us at the gate.

"Ah, Sir William," he said, fussing up to father, "you're looking well. Come to knock our bowling about, eh? How do you do, Miss Joan? We're getting quite the young lady now, Sir William, eh? quite the young lady."

"How do you do, Sir Edward?" I said in my number four manner, the distant but gently tolerant. (It wants practice, but I can do it quite well now.)

"I hear you have a new professional this year," said father. "Which is he?"

"Ah, yes, yes; Simpson. You have probably seen his name in the papers. He did well for Sussex last season.

There he is, standing by the tent. That tall young fellow."

I eyed Mr. Simpson with interest. He was a nice-looking young man, but gloomy. He was like a man with a secret sorrow. And I don't wonder. I suppose a bowler hates to have to bowl badly on purpose. And there was the ten pounds, too. But he must have thought it worth while, or he wouldn't have done it. I could not help wondering what was Saunders's particular attraction. Perhaps I don't see her at her best, reflected over my head in the looking-glass.

Much Middlefold won the toss, and father and another man went in to bat. I was awfully excited. I was afraid, when it actually came to the point, Mr. Simpson's blood would be up to such an extent that he would forget all about Saunders's attractiveness. The other man took the first ball.

I could see that he was very much afraid of Mr. Simpson. He looked quite green. He made a huge swipe at the ball and missed it, but it didn't hit the wickets. Then he hit one right into Sir Edward's hands, and Sir Edward let it fall and puffed out his cheeks as if he was annoyed, as I suppose he was. And then Mr. Simpson bowled very fast, and knocked two of the stumps out of the ground.

"It isn't playing the game, don't you know," I heard one of our side say, "bringing a man like Billy Simpson into a country cricket match." He was sitting on the grass not far from me with his pads on. He looked very unhappy. I suppose he was going in to bat soon. "He's too good, don't you know. We shall all be out in half an hour. It spoils all the fun of the thing. They wouldn't like it if we got a lot of first-class pros to come and bat for us. Tell you what—it's a beastly shame!"

The next man missed his first ball; it went past the wicket-keeper. They ran one run, so that now father had to bat against Mr. Simpson.

"If old Romney doesn't do something," said the man who thought Mr. Simpson too good for country cricket, "we're in the cart. He used to be a rattling bat in his time, and he might stop the rot."

He did. I was watching Mr. Simpson very carefully, but I couldn't see that he bowled any differently to father. Still, he must have done, because father hit the ball right into the tent, close to where I was sitting. And the next ball, which was the last of the over, he hit to the boundary again. Everybody clapped hard, and the man sitting on the grass near me said that, if he could keep it up, he would "knock Billy off his length, and then they'd have to have a change."

"And then," said he, "we'll have them on toast."

The match went on in a jerky sort of way. That is to say, father continued to score as if the bowling was the easiest he had ever seen, and the others simply went to the wickets and were instantly destroyed by Mr. Simpson.

"The fact is," said the young man near me, cryptically, "we're all rabbits, and old Romney is the only man on the side who could hit a football." He had himself been in, and been bowled second ball.

The last man was now at the wickets, and it was getting frightfully exciting, for father had made forty-eight. The whole score was only ninety-three. Everybody hoped that the last man would stop in long enough to let father make his fifty—especially myself.

I was in such a state of suspense that I dug quite a trench with my parasol. I felt as if I were going to faint.

The other bowler, not Mr. Simpson, was bowling. Father was batting, and he had the whole six balls to make his two runs off.

This bowler had not taken any wickets so far, and I could see that he meant to get father, which would be better than bowling any number of the rabbits, as the young man called them. And father, knowing that he was near his fifty, but not knowing quite how near, was playing very carefully. So it was not till the fifth ball of the over that he managed to make anything, and then it was only one. So now he had made forty-nine. And then that horrid, beastly idiot of a last man went and spooned up the easiest catch, and Sir Edward Cave, of all men, caught it.

I went into a deserted corner and *bellowed*.

Oh, but it was all right after all, because father said that forty-nine not out against one of the best bowlers in England was enough for his simple needs, and that, so far as our bargain was concerned, it should count as fifty.

So I am going to town for the winter, and Mr. Simpson has got his ten-pound note, and will marry Saunders, I suppose, if he hurries and manages it before the football season comes; and father is as pleased as possible with his forty-nine, because he says it restores his faith in himself and relieves him of a haunting fear that he was becoming a veteran; and the entire servants' hall is moaning with envy at Saunders's blue chiffon hat with pink roses.

—Strand, July 1905

2. Petticoat Influence

MY brother Bob sometimes says that if he dies young or gets white hair at the age of thirty it will be all my fault. He says that I was bad at fifteen, worse at sixteen, while "present day," as they put it in the biographies of celebrities, I am simply awful. This is very ungrateful of him, because I have always done my best to make him a credit to the family. He is just beginning his second year at Oxford, so, naturally, he wants repressing. Ever since I put my hair up—and that is nearly a year ago now—I have seen that I was the only person to do this. Father doesn't notice things. Besides, Bob is always on his best behaviour with father.

Just at present, however, there was a sort of truce. I was very grateful to Bob because, you see, if it had not been for him I should not have thought of getting Saunders to make Mr. Simpson let father hit his bowling about in the match with the Cave men, and then father wouldn't have taken me to London for the winter, and if I had had to stay at Much Middlefold all the winter I should have pined away. So that I had a great deal to thank Bob for, and I was very kind to him till he went back to Oxford for the winter term; and I was still on the lookout for a chance of paying back one good turn with another.

We had taken a jolly house in Sloane Street from October, and I was having the most perfect time. I'm afraid father was hating it, though. He said to me at dinner one night, "One thousand five hundred and twenty-three vehicles passed the window of the club this morning, Joan."

"How do you know?" I asked.

"I counted them."

"Father, what a waste of time!"

"Why, what else is there to do in London?" he said.

I could have told him millions of things, but I suppose if you don't like London it isn't any fun looking at the sort of sights I like to see.

The morning after this, when father had gone off to his club—to count cabs again, I suppose—I got a letter from Bob.

"DEAR KID" (he wrote) — "Just a line. Hope you're having a good time in London. I can't come down for Aunt Edith's ball on your birthday, as they won't let me. I tried it on, but the Dean was all against it. Look here, I want you to do something for me. The fact is, I've had a lot of expenses lately, with my twenty-firster and so on, and I've had rather to run up a few fairly warm bills here and there, so I shall probably have to touch the governor for a trifle over and above my allowance. What I want you to do is this: keep an eye on him, and if you notice that he's particularly bucked about anything one day, wire to me first thing. Then I'll run down and strike while the iron's hot. See? Don't forget. —Yours ever, BOB.

"P.S. There's just a chance that it may not be necessary after all. If everything goes well I may scrape into the 'Varsity team, and if I can manage to get my Blue he will be so pleased that a rabbit could feed out of his hand."

I wrote back that afternoon, promising to do all I could. But I said that at present father was not feeling very happy, as London never agreed with him very well, and he might not like to be worried for money for a week or two. He does not mind what he gives us as a rule, but sometimes he seems to take a gloomy view of things, and talks about extravagance, and what a bad habit it is to develop in one's youth, when one ought to be learning the value of money.

Bob replied that he understood, and added that a friend of his, who had it from another man who had lunched with a cousin of the secretary of football, had told him that they were thinking of giving him a trial soon in the team.

It was on the evening this letter came that Aunt Edith gave her ball. She is the nicest of my aunts, and was taking me about to places. I had been looking forward to this dance for weeks.

I wore my white satin with a pink sash, and a special person came in from Truefitt's to do my hair. He was a restless little man, and talked to himself in French all the time. When he had finished he stepped back, and threw up his hands and said, "Ah, mademoiselle, c'est magnifique!"

I said, "Yes, isn't it?"

It was, too.

I suppose different people have their different happiest moments. I expect father's is when he makes a good stroke at cricket or shoots particularly well. And Bob has his, probably, when he kicks a football farther than anybody else. At least, I suppose so. I love cricket, but I don't understand football. At any rate, I know when I feel happiest. It is when I know I look nice and when the floor is just right and I have a partner whose step suits mine.

On this particular night everything was absolutely perfect. I looked very nice. I know one isn't supposed to be aware of this, but father and Aunt Edith both told me, as well as at least half my partners, so there was a mass of corroborative evidence, as father says. Then the floor was lovely, and everybody seemed to dance well except one young man who had come from Cambridge for the ball. He danced very badly, but he did not seem to let it weigh upon his spirit at all. He was extremely cheerful.

"Would you prefer me," he asked, "to apologize every time I tread on your foot, or shall I let it mount up and apologize collectively at the end?"

I suggested that we might sit out. He had no objection.

"As a matter of fact," he said, "dancing's good enough in its way, but footer's my game."

I said, "Oh!"

"Yes. Best game on earth, I think. I should like to play it all the year round. Cricket? Oh, yes, cricket's good enough in its way, too. But it's not a patch on footer. I was playing last week—"

My attention wandered.

"So you see," he went on, "by half time neither side had scored. We had the wind with us in the second half, so—"

I could never understand football, so I am afraid I let my attention wander again. After some minutes I heard him say, "And so we won after all. Now, you can't get that sort of thing at cricket."

I said, "I suppose not."

"Best game on earth, footer. I say, see that man who just passed us with the girl in red?"

I looked round. The man he referred to was my partner for the next dance. He was tall and wiry, and waltzed beautifully. He seemed a shy man. I noticed that he appeared to find a difficulty in talking to the lady in red. He looked troubled.

"See him?" said my companion.

I said I did.

"That's Hook."

"Yes; I remember that was his name."

My companion seemed to miss something in my manner—surprise or admiration.

"*The* Hook, you know," he added. "Captain of footer at Oxford. You must have heard of T. B. Hook!"

I didn't like to say I had not; so I murmured, "Oh, *T.*

B. Hook!"

This satisfied him. He went on to describe Mr. Hook.

"Best forward Oxford's had for seasons. See him dribble—my word! Halloa! there's the band starting again. May I take you—"

At this moment Mr. T. B. Hook detached himself—with relief I thought—from the lady in red, and, after looking about him, caught sight of me and made his way in my direction. I admired the way he walked. He seemed to be on springs.

He danced splendidly, but in silence. After making one remark to him—about the floor—which caused him to look scared and crimson, I gave up the idea of conversation, and began to think, in a dreamy sort of way, in time to the music. It was not till quite the end of the dance that my great idea came to me. It came in a very roundabout way. First I thought about father, then about Bob, then about Bob's letter, then about his saying he might play for Oxford. And then, quite in a flash, I realized that it was Mr. T. B. Hook, and no other, who had the power of letting him play or keeping him out, and I saw that here was my chance of doing Bob the good turn I owed him. I have since been told—by Bob—that an idea so awful (so absolutely fiendish, was his expression) could only have occurred to a girl. Ingratitude, as I have said before, is Bob's besetting sin.

One of my aunts is always talking about the tremendous influence of a good woman. My idea was to try it, for Bob's benefit, on Mr. T. B. Hook.

The music stopped, and we went into the

conservatory. My partner's silence was more noticeable now that we had stopped dancing. His waltzing had disguised it.

We sat down. I could *feel* him trying to find something to say. The only easy remark, about the floor, I had already made.

So I began.

I said, "You are very fond of football, aren't you?"

He brightened up.

"Oh, yes," he said. "Yes. Yes."

He paused for a moment, then added, as if he had had an inspiration, "Yes."

"Yes?" I said.

"Oh, yes," he replied, brightly. "Yes."

Our conversation was getting quite brisk and sparkling.

"You're captain of Oxford, aren't you?" I said.

"Oh, yes," he replied. "Yes."

"I'm very fond of cricket," I said, "but I don't understand football. I suppose it's a very good game?"

"Oh, yes. Yes."

"I have a brother who's a very good player," I went on.

"Yes?"

"Yes. He's at Oxford, too. At Magdalen."

"Yes?"

"Are you at Magdalen?"

"Trinity."

"Do you know my brother?"

I saw he hadn't heard my name when we had been

introduced, so I added, "Romney."

"I don't think I know any Romney. But I don't know many Magdalen men."

"I thought you might, because he told me you were probably going to put him into the Oxford team. I do hope you will."

Mr. Hook, who had been getting almost at home and at his ease, I believe, suddenly looked pink and scared again. I heard him whisper, "Good Lord!"

"Please put him in," I went on, feeling like Bob's guardian angel. "I'm sure he's much better than anybody else, and we *should* be so pleased."

"You would be so pleased," he repeated, mechanically.

"*Awfully* pleased," I said. "I couldn't tell you how grateful. And it would make such a lot of difference to Bob. I can't tell you why, but it would."

"Oh, it *would?*" said he.

"A tremendous lot. You won't forget the name, will you? Romney. I'll write it down for you on your programme. R. Romney, Magdalen College. You *will* put him in, won't you? I shall be too grateful for anything. And father—"

"I think this is ours?" said a voice.

My partner for the next dance was standing before me. In the ball-room they were just beginning the Eton boating song. I heard Mr. Hook give a great sigh. It may have been sorrow, or it may have been relief.

About a week after this father said "Halloa!" as he was reading the paper at breakfast. "They're playing Bob at half for Oxford, Joan," he said, "against Wolverhampton

Wanderers."

"Oh, father!" I said; "are they really?"

The influence of the good woman had begun to work already.

"Instead of Welby-Smith, apparently. I suppose they had to make some changes after their poor show against the Casuals. Well, I hope Bob will stay in now he's got there."

"You'd be pleased if he got his Blue, wouldn't you, father?"

"Yes, my dear, I should."

I thought of writing to Mr. Hook to thank him, but decided not to. It was best to let well alone.

I got a letter from Bob a fortnight later saying that he was still in the team, though he had not been playing very well. He himself, he said, had rather fancied he would have been left out after the Old Malvernians' match, and he wouldn't have complained, because he had played badly; but for some reason they stuck to him, and if he didn't do anything particularly awful in the next few matches, he said, he was practically a certainty for Queen's Club.

"What's Queen's Club?" I asked father.

"It's where the 'Varsity match is played. We must go and see it if Bob gets his Blue. Or in any case."

Bob did get his Blue. I felt quite a thrill when I thought of what Mr. Hook had suffered for my sake. Because, you see, there were lots of people who thought Bob wasn't good enough to be in the team. Father read me a bit out of a sporting paper in which the man who wrote it compared the two teams and said that "the weak spot in the Oxford side is undoubtedly Romney," and a lot of horrid things about his not feeding his forwards properly. I said, "I'm sure that isn't true. Bob's always giving dinners to people. In fact, that's the very reason why—"

I stopped.

"Why what?" said father.

"Why he's so hard up, father, dear. He is, you know. It's because of his twenty-first birthday, he said."

"I shouldn't wonder, my dear. I remember my own twenty-first birthday celebrations, and I don't suppose things have altered much since my time. You must tell Bob to come to me if he is in difficulties. We mustn't be hard on a man who's playing in the 'Varsity match, eh, my dear?"

I said, "No; I'll tell him."

Bob stopped with us the night before the match. He hardly ate anything for dinner, and he wanted toast instead of bread. When I met him afterwards, though, he was looking very pleased with things and very friendly.

"It's all right about those bills," he said. "The governor has given me a cheque. He's awfully bucked about my Blue."

"And it was all me, Bob," I cried. "It was every bit me. If it hadn't been for me you wouldn't be playing to-morrow. Aren't you grateful, Bob? You ought to be."

"If you can spare a moment and aren't too busy talking rot," said Bob, "you might tell me what it's all about."

"Why, it was through me you've got your Blue."

"So I understand you to say. Mind explaining? Don't, if it would give you a headache."

"Why, I met the Oxford captain at Aunt Edith's dance, and I said how anxious you were to get your Blue, and I begged him to put you in the team. And the very next Saturday you were tried for the first time."

Bob positively reeled, and would have fallen had he not clutched a chair. I didn't know people ever did it out of novels. He looked horrible. His mouth was wide open and his face a sort of pale green. He bleated like a sheep.

"Bob, *don't!*" I said. "Whatever's the matter?"

He recovered himself and laughed feebly. "All right, Kid," he said, "that's one to you. You certainly drew me then. By gad! I really thought you meant it at first."

My eyes opened wide. "But, Bob," I said, "I did."

His jaw fell again.

"You mean to tell me," he said slowly, "that you actually asked—Oh, my aunt!"

He leaned his forehead on the mantelpiece.

"I shall have to go down," he moaned. "I can't stay up after this. Good Lord! the story may be all over the 'Varsity! Suppose somebody did get hold of it! I couldn't live it down."

He raised his head. "Look here, Joan," he said; "if a single soul gets to hear of this I'll never speak to you again." And he stalked out of the room.

I sat down and cried.

He would hardly speak a word to me next morning. Father insisted on his having breakfast in bed, so as not to let him get tired; so I did not see him till lunch. After lunch we all drove off to Queen's Club in Aunt Edith's motor. While Bob was upstairs packing his bag, father said to me, "Here's an honour for us, Joan. Bob is bringing the Oxford captain back to dinner to-night."

I gasped. I felt it would take all my womanly tact to see me through the interview. He wouldn't know how offended Bob was at being put in the team, and he might refer to our conversation at the dance.

Bob was evidently still wrapped in gloomy despair when he joined us. He was so silent in the motor that father thought he must be dreadfully nervous about the match, and tried to cheer him up, which made him worse. We arrived at the ground at last, and Bob went to the pavilion to change.

We sat just behind two young men whose whole appearance literally shrieked the word "Fresher"! When I thought that Bob had been just like that a year before and that he was really quite different now, I felt so proud of my efforts to improve him that I was quite consoled for the moment. I was in a gentle reverie when father nudged me, and I woke up to find that the two young men were discussing Bob. "Yes, that's all very well," one of them was saying, the one in the brighter brown suit, "but my point is that he's too selfish. He doesn't feed his forwards enough."

I wondered whether this young man had been reading the sporting paper.

"He's pretty nippy, though," said the other.

"Personally, if I had been skipper," said the bright

brown one, "I should have played Welby-Smith. Why they ever chucked him licks me."

"Well, I don't know," the other was beginning, when his words were drowned in a burst of applause, as the Cambridge team came on to the field. There was another shout a moment later, and Oxford appeared, Bob looking like a dog that's just going to be washed.

"Good," said the bright young man; "we've won the toss. The Tabs'll have to play with the sun in their eyes second half. Just when it's setting, too."

I was glad to hear this, because I know what a nuisance the sun in one's eyes is at cricket, and I suppose it must be just as bad at football.

There was a lot of running about and kicking at first. A little Cambridge man with light hair got the ball after a bit, and simply tore down the touch-line till he came to Bob, and Bob got in his way, and he kicked it to another man, only before he'd got it the other man who had been standing nearest to Bob at the beginning of the game took it away from him and sent it a long way up the field.

"Well played, Bob!" said father. "That little man with the light hair is Stevens, the international. He's the most dangerous man Cambridge have got. Bob will have his work cut out to stop him. Still, he did it that time all right."

The ball was being kicked about quite near the Cambridge goal now, so I thought Oxford must be getting the best of it. The little man was standing about by himself looking on, as if he were too important a person to mix himself up with the others. But suddenly one of the other Cambridge men sent the ball in his direction and he was off with it like a flash, and there seemed to be nobody there to stop him except Bob, who was jumping about half-way down the field.

All the Cambridge men raced down in the direction of the Oxford goal, and Bob met the little man as he had done before and made him pass to the other man. Then Bob rushed for this man, though there was another Oxford player rushing for him too, and the Cambridge man with the ball waited till they were both quite near him and then kicked it back to the international.

"Oh, Romney, you rotter!" said one of the young men in front of me, in a voice of agony; and then there was a perfect howl of joy from half the crowd, for the international, who hadn't anyone between him and the goal but the goalkeeper, who looked nervous, ran round and shot the ball through into the net. "Well, there's one of their goals," said the not quite so bright young man. "Chap writing in the *Chronicle* this morning said Oxford would be lucky if they only had three scored against them. What a rotter Romney was to leave Stevens like that! Why on earth can't he stick to his man?"

Father looked quite grey and haggard.

"If Bob's going to play the fool like that," he said, "he'd better have stayed at home."

"What didn't he do?" I asked.

"He didn't stick to his man. He gets up against an international forward, and the first thing he does is to leave him with a clear field. He must stick to Stevens."

The whole air seemed full of Bob's wrongdoing. I

suppose it was a sort of wireless telegraphy or something that made me do it. At any rate, I jumped up and shrieked in front of everybody, in a dead silence, too: "*You must stick to Stevens, Bob!*"

Then there was a roar of laughter. I suppose it must have sounded funny, though I didn't mean it; and everybody who wanted Oxford to win took up the cry. Only after shouting, "You must stick to Stevens, Bob!" once, they began to shout, "Buck up, Oxford!"

Bob turned scarlet—I was looking at him through father's field-glasses—and I believe he was swearing to himself. Then the game began again.

Bob told me afterwards, in a calmer moment, that my cry was the turning-point. Up to then he had been fearfully ashamed of himself for letting the Cambridge man kick the ball away from him, but that now he felt that he must look so foolish that it was not worth while trying to realize it. He said he was like the girl in Shakespeare who smiled at grief. He had passed the limits of human feeling. The result was that he found himself suddenly icy cool, without nerves or anxiety or anything. He isn't good at explaining his feelings, but I think I understand what he meant. I have felt it sometimes myself when, directly after I have had my best dress trodden on and torn at a dance, I have gone down to supper and found that all the meringues have been eaten. It is a sort of calm, divine despair. You know nothing else that can happen to you can be bad enough in comparison to be worth troubling about.

Anyhow, the result was that Bob began to play really

splendidly. I can't judge football at all, of course, but even I could see how good he was. He slipped about as if he were made of India rubber. He sprang at Stevens and took the ball away from him. He kept kicking the ball back to the Cambridge goal. In fact, he thoroughly redeemed himself, and if it hadn't been for the Cambridge goalkeeper Oxford would have scored any number of times. Just before half-time an Oxford man did score, so that made them level.

"Well, Romney's done all right lately," said one of the young men. "If he plays like that all the time we might win. What on earth he was doing at the start I can't think."

The sun was getting very low now, and Cambridge had to play facing it. It seemed to bother them a good deal, and Oxford kept on attacking, Bob coming up to help. At last, after they had been playing about twenty minutes, Stevens went off again, and Bob had to race back and stop him. He just managed to kick the ball over the touch-line. One of the Cambridge men picked it up and threw it in to another Cambridge man, but Bob suddenly darted between them, got the ball, and tore down the field. There were only two men in front of him besides the goalkeeper, and he wriggled past one of them, and father stood up and waved his hat and shouted instructions. Then the last Cambridge man bore down on him. It was thrilling. They were on the point of charging into one another when Bob kicked the ball to the left and ran to the right, and the Cambridge man shot past, and there was Bob in front of the goal just getting ready to shoot. Then the ball whizzed into the net, and all over the ground you could see hats flying into the air and sticks waving and a great roar went up from everywhere. It sounded like guns. "All the same," said the bright brown young man, "he ought to have passed."

Nothing more was scored, so Oxford just won.

The end was rather funny, because I know you are wondering what I said to Mr. Hook and what he said to me, and what Bob did.

But it wasn't a bit like what I had expected. When I came down to the drawing-room after dressing for dinner Bob and the captain were standing talking by the fire.

"I think you have met my sister already," said Bob, dismally.

"I don't think I've had the pleasure," murmured the other man.

Bob turned to me.

"I thought you said you met Watson at Aunt Edith's ball. So you *were* pulling my leg after all?"

"I didn't. I wasn't. I said I met the captain of the Oxford football team."

"Well, that's Watson."

"Are you captain, really?" I asked.

"I've always been told so."

"Then," I said, "I think it's my duty to tell you that there is a man called Hook—T. B. Hook—who goes about pretending *he's* captain."

"Hook of Oriel? Rather shy man? Doesn't talk much?"

"Yes."

"Oh, he's captain of the Oxford Rugger team, you see.

I'm captain of the Soccer," said Mr. Watson.

"So it was Hook you asked?" said Bob. "Thank Heaven. You haven't ruined my career, after all. Though I admit," he added, kindly, "you did what you could."

It is curious how everything seems to be all for the best. You would have thought that all my trouble had been wasted. But next day, to show his relief, Bob took me out and used some of father's cheque in buying me the loveliest white "feathery" on earth; showing that out of evil cometh good, as our curate at home says.

—Strand, February 1906

3. Personally Conducted

I SHOULD like to start by saying that all this happened two days after my sixteenth birthday, when my hair was still down, so that I hadn't anything to live up to, and it didn't matter what I did—or not much, at any rate. That's how it was.

It all began at breakfast on the Saturday. We were going to play Anfield that afternoon. Anfield is a town a few miles off, and the match is one of the best that Much Middlefold plays. So that I wasn't surprised that father was annoyed when he got the curate's letter. He opened it at breakfast, just after I had come down. I was pouring out the coffee when I heard him snort in the way he always does when anything goes wrong.

I said, "What's the matter, father dear?"

"Here's a nice thing," he said, waving the letter. "Morning of match—most important match—team not any too strong—wanting everyone we can possibly get, and here's Parminter writing to say that he can't play!"

"Can't play?"

Mr. Parminter was our best bowler. He had nearly got his blue at Cambridge. Father once told me that the Vicar advertised for a curate, and said that theology didn't matter, but he must have a good break from the off; and I thought it was true till I happened to find an old number of *Punch* with the same thing in. But, anyhow, Mr. Parminter had got a break from the off. Whenever we won a match it was nearly always through his bowling. He bowled very fast. A man we know once said that there was much too much devil in his bowling, considering that he was a clergyman.

"Why can't he play?" I asked.

"The wretched man," said father, "was at the school treat yesterday, and fell out of the swing and sprained his right wrist. Would have let me know last night, he says, but thought it might be better in the morning. Finds it impossible to move his arm without considerable pain; is dictating this letter to his housekeeper, and hopes that I shall be able to fill his place without difficulty, even at such short notice. Fill his place, indeed! And I hear that Anfield are strong in batting this year, though weak in bowling."

"What are you going to do?"

"I suppose we must play young Hardy. He's quite incompetent, but he is the only one. Unless you can think of anybody else, Joan?"

I thought.

"No," I said, "I can't, father."

And it was not till the end of breakfast that I did. And even then I wasn't sure that he would be able to play. The person I thought of was my cousin—or, rather, he's only a sort of cousin, about twice removed. His name was Alan Gethryn, and he was at school at Beckford, which is quite near to us, if you bicycle. He had sometimes been to stay with us on Visiting Sundays. I knew he was good, because he had taken a lot of wickets for the Beckford team in matches. So I suggested him.

Father brightened up.

"That's an uncommonly good idea, Joan," he said. "Beckford always have a pretty useful sort of side—they coach 'em well there—and if Alan's in the team he ought to be a decent player."

"He's in the team all right," I said. "He was top of the bowling averages last year."

"This is excellent. I wonder if we could get him."

"And I could easily bike over and ask him, father," I added. "Shall I? And if he can play, I could wire to you, so that you would know in time. If he can't play, you can always get Hardy."

Father said, "Very well," so I got my bicycle, and, after sending off a wire telling Alan to meet me outside the school-gates during the quarter of an hour interval in the morning I went off. I got to the school at twenty to eleven, and rode up and down outside, and presently Alan strolled out.

"Hullo!" he said.

"I say, Alan," I said, "would you like a game this afternoon for Much Middlefold?"

"A what?" he said.

"A game. Father sent me over to ask you if you'd play. Mr. Parminter has sprained his wrist, so we want a bowler. It'll be an awfully jolly match, and you could have tea with us, and get back afterwards."

He looked thoughtful.

"Difficulty is, you see, the corps are going off on a field-day this afternoon, and I shall be in charge here. Got to take roll-call, and so on."

"When's roll-call?"

"Four."

"Oh, I say. Then you can't come?"

"Wait. Let's think this thing over. Reece would take roll-call all right if I asked him, so that disposes of that. It would be out of bounds, of course, going to your place, but I don't see who's to know. So there goes that, too. I could change here and bike over. There wouldn't be any difficulty about that. And I happen to know that Leicester is going to be out of the way all the afternoon. So it's all right. I shall be able to come."

"Oh, good!" I said. "Who's Leicester?"

"My house-master. Under ordinary circs he'd be at roll-call while I ticked off the names, and I'd have to hand the list to him then. But he was telling us this morning at breakfast that he was going to spend the afternoon looking at an old church somewhere. He's keen on antiquities, you know, and brass-rubbing, and all that sort of thing. So he won't be on hand. All I've got to do is to get back here by about six or half-past and give him the list then."

After lunch Alan came.

"Ah, Alan, my boy," said father. "Glad you were able to turn up. Had lunch? That's right. I've got to go down to meet these Anfield fellows. You come on later. We don't start till two-thirty. You know your way down to the ground, don't you? See you there."

He went out of the room, carrying his cricket-bag, and returned almost at once.

"Pretty nearly forgotten it, by gad!" he said. "I say, Joan, there's something I want you to do for me. It won't make you miss more than an over or two of the game. I met a man at the Burley-Grey's some time back, and we got talking about antiquities—seems he's keen about them—so I gave him a general invitation to come over here and let me show him over our church. He has rather unfortunately chosen to-day for his visit. I had his letter at breakfast, only this Parminter business put it out of my mind. I wish you would just show him the way to the church when he comes, Joan. He will arrive here at about three on his bicycle. Just explain that I can't possibly get away. You needn't stay with him, of course. Simply take him to the church, and leave him. He won't want conversation. He is going to rub brass, or some such thing. I don't know what he means—it doesn't sound a very amusing way of spending a fine summer's afternoon—but that is what he said. Just tell him there will be tea here at about half-past four if he cares to turn up for it. But I should not think he would."

I looked at Alan in a perfect panic. It could not be a coincidence.

"What is his name, father?" I asked. Father actually had to think before he could tell me. I could have told him at once.

"Leinster? Leicester—that's it. Leicester. Mrs. Burley-Grey introduced him to me."

Father went out again, and Alan and I were alone. I waited till I heard the front door shut.

"This," Alan said, "wants thinking out. Ginger-beer may help." He poured some into a glass and drank it, but it didn't seem to act. He offered no suggestion.

"Oh, do say *something*, Alan," I said. "What *are* we going to do? Will you go back?"

"And leave your father in the cart? Not much. I'm a fixture for the afternoon if the place was crawling with Leicesters. Am I down-hearted? No! On the other hand, it's rather a brick, this happening. The thing we want to do is to keep him off the field altogether, if possible, at any rate as long as we can. I don't see why he shouldn't be perfectly happy rubbing brass all the afternoon. Why not leave him there and risk it?"

"I couldn't. We *must* think of something better."

"Well, you have a shot. I'm getting a headache. I'll tell you one thing I'll do. I'll ask your father if he wins the toss to put them in first, as I have to leave early. That'll help a bit. Hullo, it's twenty past! I shall have to rush. I leave you in charge of this thing. Knock him on the head and tie him up. Lock him in the church and bag the keys."

I saw him to the door, and watched him bike off in the direction of the field. Then I went back to the dining-room to think it all over.

There was a ring at the front door about three o'clock, and I thought it was bound to be Mr. Leicester. A bicycle was against the pillar at the front of the steps, and a thin, elderly man was standing on the top one, leaning down and picking trouser-clips off himself. He stood up when I opened the door, and looked at me inquiringly through a pair of gold-rimmed glasses. He had a very mild, kind face, rather like a sheep.

"Oh, are you Mr. Leicester?" I said. "Because father's very sorry he's had to go off to the match—we're playing Anfield to-day—and I'm going to show you to the church."

"I shall be very much obliged, if it would not be giving you too much trouble. I fear I have called at an inconvenient time."

He had, of course, but I couldn't say so.

I said, politely, "Not at all."

We put his bicycle in the stables and set off across the fields to the church, about half a mile away.

Mr. Leicester didn't talk much while we were walking. I think he didn't quite know what to say to me. And I was wondering so much what I was to do to keep him from meeting Alan that I didn't talk much either.

When we got in sight of the church he brightened up.

"How very beautiful!" he said, standing quite still and pointing, like a dog when it smells a bird. "How picturesque! That grey stone has a delightfully soothing effect against the green of the trees, with the white road winding behind it. How truly picturesque!"

I said, "Yes, isn't it top-hole!"

He said, "I beg your pardon?"

I said, "Not at all."

And we went on.

As soon as we got inside he pointed again. I saw that he was looking at the old brass tablet at the end of the aisle, the one that was put there by the widow of a man who died in Edward III's time. He put a large piece of paper, which he had been carrying, on it, and knelt down and began to scratch at it with something black. I locked the door, and came and sat in a pew near, and watched him. He scratched and scratched away, and I sat and sat till I heard the clock strike four. I almost wished I had gone and left him, for I was dying to see the match, and I was pretty sure that he would have stopped there.

At about a quarter past four it suddenly occurred to me that there wasn't any need for me to go on sitting there, because the door was locked and I had the key, so he couldn't get out without my knowing. So I got up and began to explore. I had never been anywhere in the church except in our pew, and in the vestry, at a christening, so there was lots to see. I wandered about, and at last I saw a little door with some steps behind it. I went up and up, till I found myself looking into a great sort of loft place full of ropes, which I knew must be the belfry. The steps went on round the corner. I started off again, and came to a trap-door. I pulled this down, and there I was on the roof of the tower, with the loveliest view in front of me you ever saw.

I could see the cricket-field, with little specks of white

on it. If I had had some glasses I could have watched the match beautifully.

I sat there looking at the view till I heard a scraping on the steps, and Mr. Leicester's head bobbed up through the trap-door. He beamed at me, panting rather hard, and then pulled himself up.

"Ah! the roof!" he said. "What a delightful view! I suppose that is the cricket-field, with the little white figures beyond the stream. How delightfully cool the breeze is up here! Really, one is almost sorry to have to descend into the heat below."

I didn't like this. It sounded as if he were going.

"Why not stop up here?" I said.

"It would certainly be pleasant. But I should like to see your father before I return to Beckford. I must thank him for the great treat he has given me this afternoon in allowing me the privilege of seeing this beautiful old church."

I said, in a hurry, "Oh, it doesn't matter about father, really. I mean, of course, he may be batting or anything. He'll probably be very busy."

"I should like very much to see him bat," said Mr. Leicester benevolently.

"Aren't you going on doing the brass?" I asked.

"I think not to-day—not to-day. I find the continuous stooping a little trying for the back, and I have obtained a very satisfactory impression. I think that we had better be going down, if you have no objection."

So I dropped the keys over the parapet, and they fell with a rattle on the gravel path. It was a desperate measure, as they say in the books, but I couldn't think of anything else.

"What was that?" asked Mr. Leicester.

"Oh, I say," I said, "I'm awfully sorry. I've dropped the keys!"

"We had better go down and recover them."

"But don't you see? We can't get out. The door's locked."

Mr. Leicester's mouth opened feebly.

"We must sit here and wait for someone to come and let us out. The worst of it is everybody's at the match. Still, we can't stay here for ever, because when father finds I don't come in to dinner—"

"Dinner! In to dinner! My dear young lady, it is imperative that I should be back at Beckford at half-past six!"

"I'm awfully *sorry*," I said, "but unless somebody comes along —"

"Is there no other way out?" he asked.

"I'm afraid not," I said. "It was careless of me to drop them."

"Pray, pray do not distress yourself. These accidents happen to everyone."

I have always thought it awfully nice of him not to be angry, because he might easily have been. I know I should have been if somebody had kept me locked in a place when I wanted to get out.

"We sat and waited there for about another quarter of an hour. It was jolly awkward. I didn't know what to say. It was no good talking about the view, because he was too worried by the thought of not being able to get back in time to care much about anything else.

"I really think," he said at last, "that we had better shout for assistance."

It is all very well to make up your mind to shout for assistance, but it isn't easy to think what to shout. We both began at the same time. He cried, "Help!" I shouted "Hi!"

We didn't make very much noise really, because he had a weak voice and I didn't shout my loudest, as I was afraid of making myself hoarse. But it sounded quite loud in the stillness.

"I fear it is hopeless," said Mr. Leicester. "The neighbourhood appears completely deserted." But just then, as I was hoping that it was all right and that we shouldn't be let out till Alan had got safely home, I heard somebody shuffling along in the road, and singing. It was like the bit in "The White Company," where they're on the burning tower and can't get down and hear the archers singing the Song of the Bow in the distance. Only they were pleased, and I wasn't.

Mr. Leicester jumped up and leaned over the side and shouted quite loud. The singing stopped.

" 'Ullo! 'ullo!" said a voice, and the gate clicked. I looked over Mr. Leicester's shoulder, and saw a tramp standing below, shading his eyes with his hand.

"My good man," said Mr. Leicester, "I should be very much obliged if you would let us out."

"Wot's the little gime?" said the man.

"We are locked in, and cannot get out. You will find

the key a little to your left, lying on the gravel path. Take it and unlock the door."

The tramp was a man of business.

"Wot do I make outer this?" he wanted to know.

"I will give you a shilling," said Mr. Leicester.

" 'Arf a dollar, guv'nor, 'arf a dollar. Liberty, the bloomin' 'eritage of the bloomin' Briton, thet's wot I'm going to give yer. It's cheap at 'arf a dollar."

"Very well," said Mr. Leicester.

We went down the steps, and presently we heard the key in the lock and the door opened.

I wasted as much time as possible walking home, and we did not get to the field till about half-past five. I was faint for want of tea. Father and Thoms, the son of the vicar's gardener, were batting. Just as we came on to the ground father hit a beautiful four to leg. I raced on ahead of Mr. Leicester to warn Alan. I found him in the pavilion—at least, we call it a pavilion; it's really only a sort of shed. There are two floors. On the top one the scorer sits, but not often anybody else. Alan was there, with his pads on.

"Hullo!" he said, "what a time you've been. What have you been doing? Where's Leicester?"

I told him all about it in a whisper, so that the scorer shouldn't hear. He seemed to think it funny, but he remembered to thank me. If he hadn't, after all I had been through, I don't know what I should have done.

"Where's he now?" he asked.

"He would come here with me. He's somewhere on the ground."

"That's rather awkward. Half a second! I'll go down and spy out the land."

He went down the ladder, but came up again almost at once. He shut down the trap-door very quietly, and came and sat at the back of the room.

"That was a close thing," he said, grinning. "He's sitting on a bench down there, watching the game. I nearly charged into him."

"What are you going to do?"

"Sit tight. That's the programme at present. I say, though, this is about the tightest place I've ever been in. I'm in next! Bit awkward, isn't it? If either Thoms or your pater gets out, I'm pipped; I must go down. But perhaps he won't stop."

"He will," I said miserably. "He's waiting to see father, to thank him for asking him to come to the church."

Alan grinned again. I really believe he enjoyed it.

"Well, I don't see that we can do anything. It's just possible that your pater may knock off the runs. He's playing a ripping game."

"It's the other man I'm worried about," said Alan. "He's a rabbit from the old original hutch. Look at him scratching away at the fast man."

I looked at him and wondered why they could not get him out. Every ball seemed to go just above or just to one side of the wicket. Then it was the end of the over, and father had the bowling. The first ball was a full-pitch, and he hit it right into the shed. We could hear it bumping against things down below.

"Well hit, sir," said Alan. "Let's hope that's killed

Leicester."

Somebody threw the ball back. The bowler bowled again, and father drove it over his head. They got three for it.

"Oh, don't run odd numbers," said Alan. "Now the rabbit's got the bowling, and he'll be shattered to a certainty."

Every ball looked as if it was going to bowl that wretched Thoms. The first two hopped over his wicket. The next was to leg, and he swiped at it but missed. The last of the over was a half volley. He mowed at it, and it hit the top of his bat and up it went into the air, the easiest catch for point you ever saw.

Alan got up with a resigned expression, and began to take off his blazer.

"He can't miss *that*," he said. "The young hero will now walk with a firm step to his doom."

Point was standing with his hands behind his back and a smile on his face, waiting for the ball to come down. It came, and he—missed it. I was quite sorry for him, especially as all the village boys shouted and jeered. (They *will* do it. We can't get them not to.)

"I shouldn't have thought," said Alan, sitting down again, "that a man could drop a sitter like that if he'd been paid for it. Now it ought to be all right."

"What are you going to do about getting back?" I asked. "If you both start at the same time he's sure to see you."

"That's true. I'd forgotten that. This business seems to develop difficulties while you wait. Where's his bike?"

"In the stables."

"Mine's just round behind the pav. So I shall get a sort of start. Can't you keep him hanging about a bit, till I've got well off?"

"I'll try."

A ripping idea suddenly occurred to me. I got up.

"Where are you off to?" asked Alan.

"The stables," I said. "Good-bye. I shan't see you again before you go. Thanks awfully for playing."

"Thanks for the game. Jolly good game. There's another four. Only six to win now."

I went down the ladder and ran across the ground. When I got to the gate I heard tremendous yelling from the village boys, and I saw them all going back to the pavilion, so I knew that we had won.

After I had been to the stables, I went back to the field, and met father and Mr. Leicester coming to our house. They had just passed the lodge gates.

"Well, Joan," said father, "we won, you see, thanks to——"

I said, quickly: "Thanks to you, father dear. Didn't he bat well, Mr. Leicester?"

"Exceedingly vigorously," said Mr. Leicester. "Exceedingly vigorously. But I must really hurry away. We left the bicycle in the stables, did we not?"

But when we got to the stables we found the back tyre absolutely flat.

Mr. Leicester's face lengthened.

"How very unfortunate," he said.

"Great nuisance," said father.

I said, "What an awful pity!"

"Particularly," said Mr. Leicester, "as I omitted to bring my repairing outfit with me. It was a deplorable oversight."

"Oh, that's all right," said father. "My daughter has whatever you will want. Run along and get the things, Joan."

It was about ten minutes before I got back. I found them looking at the bicycle in silence. I put down the repairing stuff. Then I said, "You know, it may not be a puncture, after all. Perhaps the valve has worked loose. Mine sometimes does."

"I hardly think," said Mr. Leicester, "that that can be the—why, yes, you are perfectly right: it is quite loose. I wonder how that can have happened?"

I said, "I wonder."

—Cassell's July 1907

4. Ladies and Gentlemen *v.* Players

QUITE without meaning it, I really won the Gentlemen *v.* Players match the summer I was eighteen. They don't say anything about me in the reports, but all the time I was really the thingummy—the iron hand behind the velvet glove, or something. That's not it, but it's something of that sort. What I mean is, if it hadn't been for me, the Gentlemen would never have won. My cousin Bill admits this, and he made a century, so he ought to know.

I cut the report of the match out of the *Telegraph*. The part where I come into it begins like this: "... After lunch, however, a complete change came over the game. A change frequently comes over a game of cricket after lunch; but it is usually to the disadvantage of the batting side. In this case, however, the reverse happened. Up to the interval the Gentlemen, who had gone in to make three hundred and fourteen in the fourth innings of the match, had succeeded in compiling one hundred and ten, losing in the process the valuable wickets of Fry, Jackson, Spooner, and MacLaren. As N. A. Knox, who had been sent in first on the previous evening to play out the twenty minutes that remained before the drawing of stumps, had succumbed to a combination of fading light and one of Hirst's swervers in the last over on Friday, the Gentlemen, with five wickets in hand, were faced with the task of notching two hundred and four runs in order to secure the victory. At lunch-time the position seemed hopeless. Two hundred and four is not a large score as scores go nowadays; but against this had to be placed the fact that Batkins, the Sussex professional, who had been drafted into the team at the eleventh hour, was scoring the proverbial success which attends eleventh-hour choices. From the Press Box, indeed, his bowling during the half-dozen overs before lunch appeared literally unplayable. The ball with which he dismissed MacLaren must have come back three inches. The wicket, too, was giving him just that assistance which a fast bowler needs, and he would have been a courageous man who would have asserted that the Gentlemen might even yet make a game of it. Immediately upon the re-start, however, the fortunes of the game veered completely round. Batkins' deliveries were wild and inaccurate, and the two batsmen, Riddell and James Douglas, speedily took advantage of this slice of luck. So much at home did they become that, scoring at a rapid rate, they remained together till the match was won, the Oxonian making the winning hit shortly before a quarter to six. The crowd, which was one of the largest we have ever seen at a Gentlemen *v.* Players match, cheered this wonderful performance to the echo. Douglas, the alteration in whose scholastic duties enabled him for the first time to turn out for the Gentlemen, made a number of lovely strokes in the course of his eighty-one. But even his performance was eclipsed by Riddell's great century. Without giving the semblance of a chance, he hit freely all round the wicket, two huge straight drives off successive balls from Batkins landing among the members' seats. When next our cousins from 'down under' pay us a visit, we shall be surprised if Riddell does not show them ...."

The rest is all about what Bill will do when he plays against Australia. Riddell is Bill. He is Aunt Edith's son. He is at New College, Oxford. Father says he is the best bat Oxford have had since he was up. But if you had seen him at lunch that day, you would never have dreamed of his making a century, or even double figures.

If you read what I wrote once about a thing that happened at our cricket week, you will remember who Batkins is. He came down to play for Sir Edward Cave's place against Much Middlefold last year, and got everybody out except father, who made forty-nine not out. And he didn't get father out because I got my maid Saunders, whom he was in love with, to get him to bowl easy to father so that he could make fifty. He didn't make fifty, because the last man got out before he could; but it was all right. Anyhow, that's who Batkins was.

Perhaps you think that I tried the same thing again,

and got Saunders to ask him to bowl easy to my cousin Bill in the Gentlemen *v.* Players match. But I didn't. I don't suppose he would have bowled badly in a big match like that for anyone, even Saunders.

Besides, he and Saunders weren't on speaking terms at the time.

And that's really how the whole thing happened.

I really come into the story one night just before I was going to bed. Saunders was doing my hair. I was rather sleepy, and I was half dozing, when suddenly I heard a sort of curious sound behind me—a kind of mixture of a sniff and a gulp. I looked in the glass, and there was the reflection of Saunders with a sort of stuffed look about the face. Just then she looked up, and our eyes met in the glass. Hers were all reddy.

I said: "Saunders!"

"Yes, miss."

"What's the matter?"

"Matter, miss? Nothing, miss."

"Why are you crying?"

She stiffened up and tried to look dignified. I wish she hadn't, because she was holding a good deal of my hair at the time, and she pulled it—hard.

"Crying, miss! I wouldn't demean myself—no, I wouldn't."

So I didn't say anything more for a bit, and she went on brushing my hair.

After about half a minute there was another gulp. I turned round.

"Look here, Saunders," I said, "you might as well tell

me. You'll hurt yourself if you don't. What *is* up?"

(Because Saunders had always looked after me, long before I had my hair up—when I had it right down, not even tied half-way with a black ribbon. So we were rather friends.)

"You might say. I won't tell a soul."

Then there was rather a ghark. A ghark is anything that makes you feel horrid and uncomfortable. It was a word invented by some girls I know, the Moncktons, and it supplied a long-felt want. It is a ghark if you ask somebody how somebody else is, and it turns out that they hate them or that they're dead. If you hurt anybody's feelings by accident, it is a ghark. This was one, because Saunders suddenly gave up all attempt at keeping it in, and absolutely howled. I sat there, not knowing what to do, and feeling wretched.

After a bit she got better, and then she told me what was the matter. She had had a quarrel with Mr. Batkins, and all was over, and he had gone off, and she had not seen him since.

"*I* didn't know, miss, he'd take on so about me talking to Mr. Harry Biggs when we met in the village. But he says: 'Ellen,' he says, 'I must ask you to choose between that'—then he called him names, miss—'and me.' 'William,' I says to him, 'I won't *'ave* such language from no man, I won't,' I says, 'not even if he *is* my *fiancé*,' I says. So he says: 'Promise me you won't speak to him again.' So I says: 'I won't, and don't you expect it.' 'Won't what ?' he says, 'won't speak?' 'No,' I says, 'won't promise.' 'Ho!' he says, 'so this is the end, is it? All's over, is it?' So

I says: 'Yes, William Batkins,' I says, 'all *is* over; and here's your ring what you gave me, and the photograph of yourself in a locket. And very ugly it is,' I says; 'and don't you come 'anging round me again,' I says. And so he rushed out and never came back."

She broke down once more at the thought of it.

This was the worst ghark I had ever had: because I couldn't think how I could make the thing better.

"Why don't you write to him?" I asked.

"I wouldn't demean myself, miss. And I don't know his address."

"He plays for a county, so I suppose a letter addressed care of the county ground would reach him. I remember being told which county, but I've forgotten it. Do you know?"

"No, miss. He told me it was a first-class one, but I don't remember which it was."

"Well, I'll look at the paper to-morrow, and see. He is sure to be playing."

But though I looked all through the cricket page, I could not find him.

That was Wednesday. On Thursday, my brother Bob arrived from London, bringing with him a friend of his, a Mr. Townend, who said he was an artist, but I had never seen any of his pictures. He explained this at dinner. He said that he spent the winter thinking out schemes for big canvases, and in the summer he was too busy playing cricket to be able to get to work on them.

"I say, we've been up at Lord's to-day," he said. He was a long, pleasant-looking young man, with a large smile and unbrushed hair. "Good game, rather. Er—um—Gentlemen'll have all their work cut out to win, I think."

" Ah!" said father. "Gentlemen *v.* Players, eh? My young nephew Willie is playing. Been doing well for Oxford this season—W. B. Riddell."

"Oh, I say, really? Good field. Players batted first. Fiery wicket, but it'll wear well, I think. Er—um—Johnny Knox was making them get up at the nursery end rather, but Tyldesley seems to be managing 'em all right. Made fifty when we left. Looked liked stopping. By the way, friend of yours was playing for the pros—Billy Batkins, the Sussex man. Bob was telling me that you knocked the cover off him down here last summer."

Father beamed.

"Oh!" he said. "Good deal of luck in it, of course. I managed to make a few."

"Forty-nine not out," I said, "and a splendid innings, too."

"Oh, I say, really?" said Mr. Townend, stretching out a long, thin hand in the direction of the strawberries. "Takes some doing, that. You know, they only put him into the team at the last moment. But if anyone's going to win the match for them, it'll be he. Just suit him, the wicket ought to, on the last day."

"Regular Day of Judgment for the Gentlemen," said Bob. "Somebody ought to run up to town and hold Bill's hand while he bats, to encourage him."

I said: "Father, mayn't I go up to London to-morrow? You know Aunt Edith said only the other day that she wished you would let me. And I *should* like to see Bill bat."

Father looked disturbed. Any sudden proposal confuses him. And I could see that he was afraid that if I went, he might have to go too. And he hates London.

I didn't say anything more just then; but after dinner, when Bob and Mr. Townend were playing billiards, I went to his study and asked him again.

"I should love to go," I said, sitting on the arm of his chair. "There's really no need for you to come, if you don't want to. Saunders could go with me."

"It's uncommonly short notice for your aunt, my dear," said father doubtfully.

"*She* won't mind. She's always got tons of room. And she said come whenever I liked. And Bill would be awfully pleased, wouldn't he?"

"Only make him nervous."

I said: "Oh, no. He'd like it. Well, may I?"

I kissed father on the top of the head, and he said I might.

So next day up I went with Saunders, feeling like a successful general.

I got there just before dinner. I found my cousin Bill rather depressed. He had come back from Lord's, where the Gentlemen had been getting the worst of it. The Players had made three hundred and thirty something, and the Gentlemen had made two hundred and twenty-three. Then the Players had gone in again and made two hundred and six, which wasn't good, Bill said, but left the Gentlemen more than three hundred behind.

"And we lost one wicket to-night," he said, "for nine: and the pitch is getting beastly. We shall never get the runs."

"How many did you make, Bill?"

"Ten. Run out. And I particularly wanted to get a few. Just like my luck."

I asked Aunt Edith afterwards why Bill had been so keen on making runs in this match more than any other, and she said it was because it was the biggest match he had ever played in. But Bill told me the real reason before breakfast the next morning. He was engaged, and *she* had come to watch him play.

"And I made a measly ten!" said Bill. "If I don't do something this innings, I shall never be able to look her in the face again. And I know she thinks a lot of my batting. She told me so. It's probably been an eye-opener for her."

"Poor old Bill !" I said. "Perhaps you'll do better to-day."

"I feel as if I should never make a run again," he said.

But he did.

I thought it all over that night. Of course, the difficult part was how to let Mr. Batkins know that Saunders wanted everything to be forgiven and forgotten. Because he would be out in the field all the time.

I said to Bill: "You'll be seeing Mr. Batkins, the bowler, to-morrow, won't you?"

He said: "Yes, worse luck, I shall."

"Then, look here, Bill," I said, "will you do me a favour? I want to speak to him particularly. Can I, do you think? Can you make him come and talk to me?"

"You can take a man from the pavilion," said Bill, "but you can't make him talk. What do you want him for?"

"It's private."

"You're not after his autograph, are you?"

"Of course I'm not. Why should I want his autograph?"

"Some kids would give their eyes for it. They shoot in picture-postcards to all the leading pros, and make them sign 'em."

I said nothing, but I did not like Bill hinting that I was a kid; because I'm not. I've had my hair up more than a year now.

I said: "Well, I don't, anyhow. I simply want to speak to him."

"Shy bird, Batkins. Probably if he hears that there's a lady waiting to see him, he'll lock himself in the changing-room and refuse to come out. Still, I'll have a try. During the lunch interval would be best—just before they go on to the field."

Then I arranged it with Saunders.

I said: "I shall be seeing Mr. Batkins tomorrow, Saunders. If you like, I'll give him a note from you, and wait for an answer."

"Oh, miss!" said Saunders.

"Then you can say what you like about wanting to make it up, without the ghark of doing it to his face. And if it's all right, which it's certain to be, I'll tell him to come round to Sloane Street after the match, and have some supper, and it'll all be ripping. I'm sure Aunt Edith won't mind."

Then there was another ghark. Saunders broke down again and got quite hysterical, and said I was too good to her, and she wouldn't demean herself, and she didn't know what to write, and she was sure she would never speak to him again, were it ever so, and she'd go and get the note ready now, and heaps of other things. And when she was better, she went downstairs to write to Mr. Batkins.

I believe she found it very difficult to make up the letter, because I didn't see her again that night, and she only gave it to me when we came home for lunch next day. We had decided to take Bill home in the motor to lunch, unless he had gone in in the morning and was not out, when he wouldn't have time.

We sat in the seat to the right of the pavilion. The girl Bill was engaged to was there, with her mother, and I was introduced to her. She was very anxious that Bill should make a lot of runs. She was a very nice girl. I only wished I could use my influence with Mr. Batkins, as I had done before, to make him bowl badly. But he did just the opposite. They put him on after about half an hour, and everybody said he was bowling splendidly. It got rather dull, because the batsmen didn't seem able to make any runs, and they wouldn't hit out. I thought our matches at home were much more interesting. Everybody tries to hit there.

Bill was in the pavilion all the morning; but when the umpires took the bails off, he came out to us, and we all went back in the motor. Bill was more gloomy than I had ever seen him.

"It's a little hard," he said. "Just when Hirst happens to have an off-day—he was bowling tosh this morning—and the wicket doesn't suit Rhodes, and one thinks one really has got a chance of taking a few, this man Batkins starts and bowls about fifty per cent. above his proper form. Did you see that ball that got MacLaren? It was the sort of beastly thing you get in nightmares. Fast as an express and coming in half a foot. If Batkins doesn't get off his length after lunch, we're cooked. And he's a teetotaller, too!"

I tried to cheer him up by talking about the girl he was engaged to, but it only made him worse.

"And it's in front of a girl like that," he said, "who believes in a chap, too, mind you, that I'm probably going to make a beastly exhibition of myself. That ball of Billy Batkins'll get me five times out of six. And the sixth time, too."

Saunders gave me the letter as I was going out. I reminded Bill that he had promised to get hold of Mr. Batkins for me.

"I'd forgotten," he said. "All right. When we get to the ground, come along with me."

So we left Aunt Edith in the covered seats and walked round to behind the pavilion.

"Wait here a second," said Bill. "I'll send him out. You'll have to hurry up with whatever you're going to say to him, because the Players will be taking the field in about three minutes."

I waited there, prodding the asphalt with my parasol, and presently Mr. Batkins appeared, blushing violently and looking very embarrassed.

"Did you want to see me, miss?" he said. I said "Yes," feeling rather gharked and not knowing how to begin.

"You're Mr. Batkins, aren't you?" I said at last. It was rather silly, because he couldn't very well be anybody else.

"You played against us last summer," I said, "for Sir Edward Cave, at Much Middlefold."

He started. I suppose the name made him think of Saunders.

The bell began ringing in the pavilion. He shuffled his feet. The spikes made a horrid noise on the asphalt, like a squeaking slate-pencil.

"Was there anything?" he said. "I shall have to be going out in a minute to bowl." He pronounced it as if it rhymed with "fowl."

So I saw there was no time to waste, and I plunged straight into the thing.

I said: "You know Saunders doesn't *really* care a bit for Mr. Harry Biggs. She told me so."

He turned crimson. He had been rather red before, but nothing to this.

"Me and Ellen, miss—" he began.

"Oh, I know," I said. "She has told me all about it. She's awfully miserable, Mr. Batkins. And she would have written long before, to make it up, only she didn't know your address. I've got a letter from her here, which—"

He simply grabbed the letter and tore it open. I wish I knew what was in it. He read it again and again, breathing very hard, and really looking almost as if he were going to cry.

"Can I tell Saunders it's all right?" I said.

He wouldn't answer for an age. He kept on reading the letter. Then he said: "Oh, yes, miss," very fervently. He was what Bob calls "absolutely rattled." I suppose he must have been fretting awfully all the time, really, only he wouldn't write and tell Saunders so, but let concealment, like a worm i' the bud, feed on his damask cheek.

(I used to know the whole bit once, to say by heart. I learned it when I did lessons, before I put my hair up. But I've forgotten all but that one piece now.)

"And you'll come to supper to-night? You've got the address on the letter. It's on the right-hand side of Sloane Street, as you go down."

"Oh, yes, miss. Thank you, miss."

And off he dashed in a great hurry, because the Players were just going out into the field.

So that's why "Batkins' deliveries were wild and inaccurate" after lunch. Poor man, he was so flurried by the whole thing that he could hardly bowl at all. The bowler at the other end got a man caught in his first over, and then Bill went in. And Bill hit him in all directions. It was a lovely innings. I don't think I enjoyed one more, not even father's forty-nine not out against the Cave men. They took poor Mr. Batkins off after a time, but Bill was set by then, and they couldn't get him out. He went on and on, till at last he got his century and won the match. And everybody rushed across the ground from the cheap seats, and stood by the pavilion railings, yelling. And Bill had to lean out of a window and bow.

"I withdraw what I said about friend Batkins being a teetoaller," said Bill after dinner that night to me. "No man could have bowled as rottenly as he did after lunch, on lemonade. It was the sort of stuff you get in a village game, very fast and beautifully inaccurate."

Then I told him how it had happened, and he owned that his suspicions were unjust. We were in the drawing-room at the time. The drawing-room is just over the kitchen. Bill stretched out his hands, palms downwards, and looked at the floor.

"Bless you, my children!" he said.

Bill is really an awfully good sort. When I was leaving Aunt Edith's, he came up and gave me a mysterious paper parcel. I opened it, and inside was a jeweller's cardboard box. And inside that, in cotton wool, was the duckiest little golden bat.

"A presentation bat," he explained, "because you made a century for Gentlemen *v.* Players."

—*Windsor Magazine, August 1908*

5. Against the Clock

MY family are a great anxiety to me. Sometimes when Saunders is doing my hair—it's been up for ages—nearly six months—I look in the glass, and wonder why it's not grey—the hair, I mean.

There is my brother Bob, for instance. He's much better, now, of course, for I have worked very hard on him; but when he first went to Oxford he was dreadful. He required the very firmest treatment on my part.

And even father, when my eye is not on him. There was that business of the right-of-way for example.

It happened the summer before I put my hair up. I had been away for a visit to Aunt Flora. She is one of my muddling aunts, not nearly so nice as Aunt Edith, but, on the other hand, not perfectly awful like Aunt Elizabeth. I was glad to get back.

The motor was waiting for me at the station. I sat in front instead of in the tonneau, because I wanted to talk to Phillipps, the chauffeur. He always tells me what has been happening while I have been away, and what the butler thinks about it.

To-day he started about old Joe Gossett. Joe is an old man who earns a little by winding up some of the big clocks in the village—the church clock, the one over the stables at home, and one or two more. At least, he's supposed to; but he often forgets, and then the clocks stop, and there's rather a fuss. I like Joe. He is a friend of mine. We have long talks about pigs. He loves talking about pigs. He has two of his own, and they are like sons to him. I have known him talk for three-quarters of an hour about them.

"Old Joe," said Phillipps, "he forgot to wind up the stable clock again. He's careless, Miss."

I said: "Poor Joe! Was father cross?"

Phillipps chuckled. He is the only chauffeur I have met who ever does chuckle.

"Ah!" he said. "You're right, miss. Old Joe, he's always talking about his blessed pigs, till he forgets there's anything except them in the world." Phillipps let the car go a mile before he said anything else. He's like that. He turns himself off like a tap.

He started again quite suddenly.

"Rare excitement in the village, miss, about that there right-of-way."

That was the first I had heard of it. Phillipps told me the story in jerks.

It was like this. I am condensing Phillipps' explanation, and leaving out what he said to the butler about it, and what the butler said to him.

Beyond the wood at the end of our lake is a field. The villagers have always used it as a short cut. It saved them going round two sides of a big triangle. Father didn't mind. They never went off the path, but simply walked straight from gate to gate. They had been doing it as long as I could remember. Well, father, after letting them do it for years, has suddenly said they mustn't, and closed the field. And now there was great excitement, because the villagers said that they had a legal right to use the path, and father said no, they hadn't anything of the sort, and that he had a perfect right to stop them.

I couldn't understand it a bit, because father had always been so nice to the villagers, and there didn't seem any reason for suddenly being horrid to them.

Then Phillipps explained further, and I understood.

"Mr. Morris," he said—Morris is our butler—"says that it's not, rightly speaking, the colonel's doing at all. Mr. Morris says it was Mr. Rastrick as put him up to it, and made him do it. Mr. Morris says he heard him at dinner. Mr. Morris says Mr. Rastrick kept on telling the colonel he was being put upon, and must stand up for his rights, and about the thin edge of the wedge. Mr. Morris says that what's set the colonel off."

Then I saw the whole thing, because I knew Mr. Rastrick, and knew just how he would talk father over. I hate Mr. Rastrick. He was at school with father, and sometimes comes to stay with us. He has a private school near London. My brother Bob says he bears him no grudge for that, but that what he objects to is that Mr.

Rastrick seems to look on our house as a sort of branch of his private school. He is one of those horrid men who will try to manage everybody's business. I have heard him telling Morris how to look after a cellar. He sometimes lectures Phillipps on motors. And he was always giving me advice in a horrid managing way when he was last stopping with us.

I could see him persuading father. My brother Bob once said to me that, if you were tactful, father would let you sit on his lap and help yourself out of his pockets; but that, if he got the idea that he was being let in on the quiet, he ramped.

Evidently he had ramped about this right-of-way business.

I made up my mind that I would try and stop it if I possibly could, because I know that in a day or two, when he had had time to think it over quietly, he would wish that he hadn't done it, only he would be too proud to give in then.

I thought a great deal about it as I dressed for dinner.

When I got down to the dining room, I found father and Mr. Rastrick there, and Mr. Rastrick's son, Augustus. He looked about fifteen. I had never seen him before.

"You know Joan," said father.

"Whoop-oop-oop," said Mr. Rastrick. "How you have grown! Quite the little woman, Romney, eh?"

Father beamed. I felt like scratching. I hate men who talk like aunts.

I said: "How do you do, Mr. Rastrick?" in a cold voice I usually keep for horrid boys, who forget that I have grown up, and call me by my Christian name because we used to play tennis together in some prehistoric age. It usually goes right through the boys like an east wind; but Mr. Rastrick didn't seem to notice it. He leaned against the mantelpiece and went on telling father what he ought to put on the croquet lawn in winter.

Mr. Rastrick was a tall man, with large penetrating grey eyes and a pointed black beard. He was of what they call commanding aspect. I always thought he looked like those old photographs you see in albums, where the father of the family is shown holding a scroll in one hand, apparently just about to address the multitude. Mr. Rastrick always looked as if he were just about to address the multitude. His son Augustus was short and fat. He looked to me a furtive boy. From the time I first saw him to the end of dinner he did not utter a single word, but just pounded away at his food, as if that was all he was there for. He was a little pig of a boy. Saunders, my maid, told me when he had gone that he had spent most of his visit in or near the kitchen, trying to get the cook to give him buns.

Still, it didn't matter, his being silent. His father made up for it. Between them, they talked just enough for two.

Mr. Rastrick finished off the croquet lawn before the bell rang. He took a short rest during the soup. When the fish came he started on cricket.

"Whoop-oop-oop," he began—I forgot to say he had a sort of impediment in his speech. When once he was fairly started, he talked at a tremendous rate; but he always began his speeches with those three words. It was just like a motor goes before it glides off. It was just as if somebody had started his engines.

"The young fellows nowadays," said Mr. Rastrick, beginning to glide off, "have no notion of what I call real cricket. Put them on a billiard-table, and they can play forward all day. What I like to see is the man who can make runs on a good old-fashioned village pitch. Your Frys, and Haywards, and Pulairets, where would they be on a village green? What about their three thousand runs in a season then? Why I tell you my boy Gussie would bowl them all out in a twinkling."

Gussie, who had been stuffing himself with salmon, looked round the table with his mouth full in a sort of hunted way, and remained silent.

"My boy Gussie," Mr. Rastrick went on with pride, "is a capital bowler—capital. I have trained him myself. *I* didn't let him bowl fast, like so many stupid boys. I said to him: 'Gussie, if I catch you trying to plug them in,' as I believe the expression is, 'I'll thrash you!' And I'd have done it too."

Gussie looked sad and thoughtful, as though he were brooding over painful memories.

"Whoop-oop-oop," said Mr. Rastrick enthusiastically. "Playing for my school last term against the Charchester College third eleven, an exceedingly powerful combination, including the cousin of an Oxford blue, my boy Gussie scored seven wickets for forty-six runs."

"No, did he, upon my word?" said father. "We must get up a village match for you to play in, Augustus. Seven for forty-six! By George! Excellent!"

"Whoop-oop-oop, including the cousin of an Oxford blue," said Mr. Rastrick.

"Splendid!"

The gorging boy gnawed his second helping of salmon without uttering.

It was just then that I had my idea. Do you ever notice how, when you have been thinking very hard about something, and can't decide on anything, it sometimes comes to you suddenly when you aren't thinking about it? It was just like that now. I had been trying all the time I was dressing to find some way of settling this quarrel between father and the village, and I couldn't think of anything. And now it came to me all of a sudden.

I said: "Father, I've thought of a splendid way of settling the right-of-way thing. Of course, I know they haven't any business in the field really. Still you've always let them go through it."

"Who told you about it?" asked father.

I said Phillipps had. I said: "Why not get up a match to decide it, father? It would be awful fun. If they win, let them have the right-of-way. And if we win, you could do what you liked, and shut up the field. I wish you would. Don't you think it's a good idea, father?" Because, you see, I thought the village were certain to win. Father used to be a splendid bat, and is still very good; but I didn't think we had anyone much except him, Bob being away on a cricket tour with the Authentics; and some of the village team bat very well.

I know Mr. Rastrick was just opening his mouth to say "Whoop-oop-oop, preposterous!" but it was too late.

Father always likes anything sporting, and I could see he loved this idea.

"Excellent! Capital!" he cried. "A splendid idea. I don't want to be hard on these fellows. It doesn't matter to me whether they go through the field or not. It's only the principle of the thing. I'll arrange it tonight."

"Whoop-oop-oop," began Mr. Rastrick disapprovingly; but father's mind was made up.

"Now let me see," he said. "About our team."

I must say that the House team was what Bob would have called a pretty scratch lot. Mr. Rastrick kept talking about his boy Gussie, and what he would do when he was put face to face with the village batsmen; but I thought he would have to be very good to make up for the rest. There were two grooms, three gardeners, John (the footman), Phillipps (who, Saunders told me, bowled very fast) and the curate, Mr. Travers. He was a new curate, quite different from our last one, who had once or twice played for his county. Mr. Travers had been twelfth man in his House eleven at school, he told me, but that was long ago.

I thought the village would win easily.

Our village matches at Much Middlefold are played on a meadow close to the churchyard. It is not a very nice ground—for cricket, that is to say. There is a mown space in the middle about the size of a tennis-lawn. All around it is long grass. The mown space always looks to me like a bit of ground that has been reclaimed from the jungle. The turf is not very good. It is rather rough. In a way it is a bad ground for batsmen; but then it is not very nice for the fieldsmen. There are a lot of ditches, some of them quite deep, and the long grass hides these, so that you sometimes see men running for a catch suddenly vanish. Of course, most of our regular village players have got to know where the ditches are, but they are rather a bore to strangers. Sometimes there is wet mud at the bottom of the ditches, and that makes it worse. When there isn't a match, cows are allowed onto the ground, though nobody really likes them being there; and they make a good many holes. Altogether, it is not a very good ground.

Father won the toss. And after that Mr. Rastrick seemed to appoint himself captain.

"Whoop-oop-oop," he said, "we bat first, Romney. Most certainly we bat first. You and I will be the first pair. Give the side confidence. After us anybody you like. My boy Gussie second wicket. It is his invariable place."

I scored. I generally score in our village matches. It was rather strange to-day, for the villagers, instead of crowding round, as they always do, went and sat by themselves, poor dears, at the other side of the field. I suppose they looked on me as one of the enemy. Though, of course, I was really their good angel. I was rather lonely. The curate was the only one of our team who sat by me, and he's rather a bore. Phillipps, and the grooms, and the gardeners, and John (the footman) were sitting with the maids some way off. They were all giggling and enjoying themselves tremendously.

Just before the game began, old Joe Gossett came stumping along. I hoped he was going to sit by me, but he caught sight of Mr. Travers and stumped off again.

Saunders had told me that he had forgotten to wind the church clock last week, and it had stopped and everybody was late for church, and Mr. Travers had been cross with Joe. So I suppose Joe was not anxious to see much of Mr. Travers for a little.

Of course, Mr. Rastrick took first ball. He ought to have let father take it. Father is a very good bat. Mr. Rastrick made a great fuss about taking centre, and looking round to where the fieldsmen were, and he was rather unpleasant to Harris, who always umpires in our village matches. I could not make out what it was all about, but they both waved their hands rather. Then Mr. Rastrick got settled at last, and got ready to play the first ball. And it was rather funny, because it hit him on the elbow (so he said afterwards again and again) and Hunt the grocer, who was fielding shot slip, caught it.

Everybody appealed, including the spectators, and Harris put up his hand as if he was that photograph of the Pope Blessing the World.

Mr. Rastrick had been writhing about so much that he didn't notice anything till he got ready to take the next ball—and then he saw Harris' hand. It was quite an age before they could get him to go out. He took off his pads, and went away to a corner of the field by himself, and the curate went in; so now I was left absolutely alone.

The curate was bowled by the last ball of the over, but he did not come back to talk to me. He went away by himself, like Mr. Rastrick, to a corner of the field. It is very queer about cricket. After they get out, men seem to like to go away and brood. At some of our matches I have seen half the team, dotted at intervals round the field, all brooding hard.

We had now got two wickets down for no runs. But it was father's turn to take the bowling, and he began to hit at once. He made six off his first over. Three twos. Father nearly always hits along the ground, so he never makes much more than a two when he plays on the village field.

The bowler who had got Mr. Rastrick and Mr. Travers out was Simms, the blacksmith. He is very fast. He sent our men out one after the other. The Gussie child went in after the curate, but he didn't do anything. He started running away to leg before Simms bowled (though when the ball really came it was quite slow, for Simms wouldn't bowl his fastest to a boy) and the ball hit the middle stump full pitch. Then Phillipps came in, and after making a tremendous swipe, which went right out of the ground, was caught at square leg by Payne, the baker and confectioner. I don't believe he noticed Payne was there. Payne was a very little man, and he was standing almost up to his waist in some bushes.

After that nobody did anything, hardly, except father, who played splendidly whenever he could get the bowling. The three gardeners were bowled one after the other by Simms; and if John, the footman, who went in last, hadn't had tremendous luck, and managed to stay in while father made his runs, we should have been out for about twenty. As it was, the last wicket put on eighteen before John was bowled. So our score managed to get up to forty, of which father had made twenty-three not out. There were five byes.

Of course, I thought that now it was all right, because forty was not much to expect the village to make. They often make nearly a hundred. But I had forgotten the Gussie child, or rather, I hadn't exactly forgotten him, but I didn't think he could really bowl at all. He could, though. I don't know if he was really good, but at any rate his was not the sort of bowling the village had been used to and they couldn't play it at all. Everybody in our village matches bowls either fast or very fast, so they don't mind fast bowling. They played Phillipps quite easily. But the Gussie child sent in very slow, high-pitched ones, and they swiped desperately at them, poor things, without getting anywhere near them. It would have been funny, only I was so sorry. Simms hit him into the churchyard once, but that was the only time anybody made anything off him. Simms ran himself out, and the rest just swiped, and were either clean bowled or stumped, with yells of triumph by Mr. Rastrick. The innings was over in half-an-hour for seventeen runs. The little brute Gussie took eight wickets for six.

The only thing was, there was heaps of time for a second innings. So we went in again.

It was dreadfully slow this time. Generally in our village matches everybody hits very hard, but our second innings was not a bit like that. Mr. Rastrick evidently meant to do better this innings. He simply stuck in, and didn't try to hit. Father got out quite early, caught in the slips. So did Gussie, who had gone in first wicket this time because the curate, who hadn't expected father to get out so soon, had not got his pads on. Then Mr.

Travers and Mr. Rastrick made a stand. It was too dull for anything. When five o'clock struck from the church clock, I got father to look after the scoring, while I went for a walk.

I was on my way to the house to get some tea, feeling perfectly parched, and was taking the short cut across the next field, when I suddenly thought I heard a sort of groan. And then I saw a pair of white boots sticking out from behind a bush.

I went to look.

It was the Gussie child. He was lying on the ground with his head buried in his arms, groaning hollowly. I thought he was crying.

I said: "Hello!"

He rolled over, and stared up at me in a horrid, glazed way. He wasn't crying. His face was all a sort of greeny-yellow.

I said: "What's the matter?"

He groaned and rolled over again.

Then I noticed a stump of cigar lying by his side, and I saw what had happened. I picked up the cigar. It was thick and black. I recognized what it was. The same thing had happened to Bob years ago. The cigar was one of a specially strong brand which father gives to the tenants at the tenants' dinner. He says the farmers like something with a bit of a bite in it. It looked as if Gussie had gotten bitten badly.

I didn't quite know what to do. Then I thought that he would probably sooner be left alone, so I pulled him by the shoulders till his legs didn't stick out beyond the bush, so that nobody who happened to pass should see him; and went on to the house and made myself some tea in the kitchen.

When I got back, it was twenty to six, and our side was just out. Mr. Rastrick was strutting about very pleased with himself. I looked at the score-book and found that he had carried his bat through the innings for twenty-nine. The full score was fifty-seven, which meant the villagers would have to make eighty-one to win in an hour and a quarter. I noticed one or two of them standing about looking rather sorry for themselves.

"Whoop-oop-oop," said Mr. Rastrick. "Let's get them out into the field. Play the game. The village must have their second innings. Come along, come along. Where's my boy, Gussie?"

Nobody seemed to have seen him. Everybody began to shout "Gussie!"

I stepped forward. "He's rather ill," I said. "I don't think he'll be able to bowl this innings." The faces of the village batsmen who were standing near brightened. They crowded round to listen. "Whoop-oop-oop! Why? What? Ill? What's the matter with him?"

I didn't want to get him in trouble. I said: "He may have had a touch of the sun. He's lying down." That was true, anyhow.

"Well, never mind," said father. "I'm sorry he's seedy. It has been a deuced hot day. He ought to have worn a sun hat instead of that cap. Was he quite comfortable and all right when you left him, Joan?"

I said: "He didn't seem to want to move, father."

"He's keeping quite quiet and out of the sun?"

"Yes, father."

"Then he's sure to be all right. These things pass off. We must be getting out into the field, Rastrick. Travers, will you bowl at the churchyard end?"

I saw Simms, the blacksmith, grin furtively, and I knew what he was thinking. I had seen Mr. Travers bowl sometimes at the practice net which they put up in the evenings when work is over.

"What's the time?" said father.

I looked at my watch.

"Just a quarter to six," I said.

"Whoop-oop-oop," said Mr. Rastrick authoritatively. "Now we must have no chivalry, Romney, or any of that nonsense. No playing after time's up. This is going to be a close thing. We have lost our best bowler, and they are going to try hard for the runs. There must be no playing of extra time. The rigour of the game."

"We always play by the church clock, sir," put in Simms. "We go by its strike."

"Whoop-oop-oop, quite right. Then the moment that the church clock strikes seven, off go the bails; and unless you have knocked off the runs, we win on the first innings. Umpires, do you understand that clearly? We play until the clock strikes seven, and not one instant longer."

"Right, sir," said Simms. "Ready, Teddy?"

"E-eh," said Teddy, who was the village postman. And they went in. I took the scoring-book again.

We started badly, for Mr. Rastrick, standing a long way back to Phillipps' bowling and backing with his eyes in the air to catch a skier, stepped into a deep ditch just as the ball was dropping. They ran three before he could get out again. There is a good deal of what they call the glorious uncertainty of cricket on our village ground.

After that Simms and the postman seemed to get more encouraged than ever. They hit out splendidly. I must say the bowling was awfully bad. Phillipps was all right at first, but they really liked fast bowling, and after the second over began to hit him all over the place. Mr. Travers, after four very expensive overs, was taken off, and one of the gardeners went on. He started with what I should think must have been the widest wide ever seen on a cricket field. It nearly hit Mr. Travers, who was fielding point. After that he bowled two more wides, and then at last a straight one, which Simms hit into the road.

I could see that we were not going to get the village out again. The only question was whether they could score quick enough to make the runs by seven o'clock. At half past six Simms and the postman were still in, and the score was thirty-six.

I couldn't see the clock, so I had to go by my watch, which was five minutes slow. The church clock was hidden from the field, because it had been put on the side of the tower facing the road. There was just one bit of field from which you could have seen the time, but a big yew-tree in the churchyard prevented you doing even that. So, you see, our village matches were always played by the sound of the clock, not by the sight of it. Not that it mattered much not being able to see the clock. We never had any close finishes. When the side which batted last was out, there was nearly always about three-quarters of an hour to spare.

I didn't think they could do it. You see, it had been a very hot day, and both the batsmen were beginning to be a little tired, especially Simms, who had bowled through two innings. They began to make runs more slowly. Mr. Travers, who went on instead of Phillipps, bowled a maiden. I shouldn't think he had ever done such a thing in his life. And only one run was scored off the next over from John the footman, who had gone on instead of the gardener.

It was just a quarter to by my watch, when I suddenly saw old Joe Gossett stumping towards me. He looked excited. I didn't much want him. I was afraid he was going to come and talk and I wanted to keep all my attention on the game.

He came up almost trotting.

"Hey, miss," he called out, "what's the time?"

I told him. "And my watch is slow," I said, "so it's really ten to. I don't think they'll manage it. They've only made fifty-four."

Mr. Gossett made a curious noise in the throat.

"That dratted clock hev stopped," he said, scowling at the church tower. "I should ha' wound he up yisterday to rights. I ketched sight of he as I were a-comin' down the road," he went on complainingly, "and I says, 'Surely to goodness,' I says, 'it ain't but twenty minutes past the hower.' And I says, 'If I hev'n't bin and forgot that dratted clock agen,' I says."

He was just going through the little gate into the

churchyard, near which I was sitting, when I had an idea. My brother Bob often says that girls haven't any notion of fairness and playing the game. He said it when he came back from his cricket tour at the end of the week, and I told him what I did about this match. But I said the end justified the means. And he said, "That's just the rotten sort of thing you *would* say." But I still think it did, because it would have been an awful shame if the villagers had lost their right-of-way—besides encouraging Mr. Rastrick.

Anyhow this is what I did.

I said: "Don't go away, Mr. Gossett. I haven't had anybody to talk to all the afternoon. And there's plenty of time to wind up the clock. It's only eight minutes to, so it won't be needed for another eight minutes. And nobody can see it from the field, so they won't know it's stopped." (My brother Bob, when I told him this, said, "Great Scott! And there are some people who say that women ought to have votes!")

Well, he came back; but I could see he wasn't happy. He was all nervous and jumpy, and kept asking me the time every two seconds.

So I said, "How are your pigs, Mr. Gossett?"

(When I told him that, Bob didn't utter a word. He just lifted up his head and groaned.)

Mr. Gossett's eye lit up with a sort of eager gleam. He wavered. He looked hesitatingly at the church clock and back again at me.

"Pigs," he began, and stopped.

"Pigs," I prompted gently. "I love hearing about your

pigs, Mr. Gossett."

He hesitated no longer. It all came out with a rush. He told me how pigs should be looked after, and how you ought to feed them, and what you should do when they were ill. He talked about pigs he had met. He told me how he had found one of his pigs panting one evening in his sty, and had had to spray its face for a quarter of an hour with cold water. He told me about a fight his two pigs had had. He talked about swine fever, and how to cure it. He said a good lot about bacon, and crackling, and apple-sauce.

It was all awfully interesting.

And all the while Simms and the postman were going on hitting, until, just as Mr. Gossett was beginning to give me some hints on pig-killing, the postman suddenly got out.

I suppose he must have been tired and didn't see properly, for the ball was a full-pitch, and he ought to have hit it out of the ground. As it was, it bowled him middle stump.

I said, "Oh! He's out!" and I suppose it sort of broke the spell. Anyway, Mr. Gossett stopped in the middle of a sentence and began to scramble to his feet muttering about the clock.

I didn't know what to do. The score was only seventy, and the next man in, who was Payne, the baker, was nowhere near the wicket yet. He had started to run for the crease directly the postman got out, but being so excited, he had not looked where he was going, and he was now scrambling out of the same ditch into which Mr.

Rastrick had fallen. He seemed to take hours getting out, and by the time he did, Mr. Gossett was beginning to hobble off to the churchyard gate. I couldn't stop him. He was so afraid of having it found out he had let the clock run down again that nothing would have made him wait another second.

He disappeared through the gate just as Payne got to the wickets.

Payne really wasn't the right man to send in at all, considering. He was a little shrimp of a man who just scratched about and hardly ever made a good hard hit. But just because he had gone in first wicket down in the first innings they let him do it now.

There were two more balls of the over to be bowled, and he just patted both of them. And all the time Mr. Gossett was getting nearer and nearer to the clock.

I knew there could only be one more over. As Simms was going to take it, there was just a chance. But I didn't think he could make as many as eleven.

I have never felt so excited, not even just before I went to my first grown-up dance.

The curate was bowling. Simms swiped at the first ball and missed it. The second ball he hit, but father stopped it. The third he hit very hard, but along the ground, so they only got two, because the grass stopped it. So there were nine more to make and only three balls left.

And then he missed the fourth ball.

"Whoop-oop-oop, well bowled, Travers," roared Mr. Rastrick, though it wasn't at all.

But the fifth ball was a full-pitch to leg, and Simms

sent it flying to the boundary.

And then, just as the ball had been thrown back and Mr. Travers was going to bowl, the clock struck.

Mr. Rastrick, horrid man, gave a great yell. "Whoop-oop-oop! Off with the bails, umpires! Time's up!"

And the umpires were just going to do it when father stopped them.

"Nonsense," he said. "We can't do that. We must play out the over, of course. One more ball, Simms."

Simms looked anxious but determined. Mr. Travers looked anxious too. He trotted up to the crease and bowled the last ball. And it was another full-pitch to leg. Only this time, instead of only sending it to the boundary, Simms got really hold of it. It went flying up and up, and fell with a whack right in the middle of the field—a sixer.

"By Jove!" said father, as they reached the scoring-table, "a pretty near thing. How many did Simms make? Fifty-six? Well played Simms. Capital, capital." I could see that he was as pleased as anything that the village had won. I knew that he had been thinking things over. "A thoroughly sporting game, Simms. Just tell your fellows that there will be drinks up at the house if they come on there. A wonderfully near thing. You both played splendidly, Simms. I must say, at one time I never thought you'd make the runs."

I said, "Nor did I, father."

— *Pearson's, June 1909*

Made in the USA
Middletown, DE
25 March 2015